Hard Tide

Florida Coast Adventures Book #1

Johnny Asa

ISBN: 1546790063
ISBN-13: 978-1546790068

DEDICATION

For everyone who ever wanted to sail, and even
those who didn't.

CONTENTS

CHAPTER 1

The shrill cry of the phone snapped me from a dreamless, fitful sleep. Before I could stop myself, instinct honed from years inside a warzone took over. I leapt from my bed and looked around for intruders, hand already reaching for the Buck knife in my nightstand.

As I stood there in my dark, messy studio with my heart pounding and adrenaline surging through my veins, I realized what was going on. Sweat beaded on my forehead as I turned my gaze toward my nightstand and spied my phone ringing like it was going out of style.

My eyes widened as I glanced from it to the bedside clock and back again. My dad was calling me? At 1 AM? Sure he was on East Coast time up in Florida, but it was still early for him there too.

"Weird," I muttered, reaching for the phone just as it stopped ringing.

I fruitlessly punched the answer button anyway, but it did no good. I frantically called him back. I was sure it wasn't anything, but at the same time, ever since my mom had passed away from cancer a few years back, my dad never called unless it was a birthday or a holiday. Today was neither.

"You've reached Bob Ryder. I'm not here right now, so please leave a message after the beep," his phone said the moment it connected. Hell, it hadn't even bothered to ring. Were we calling each other at the same time? Probably.

I resolved to wait a few seconds and try again. I lowered the phone and stared at it. As I did, a voicemail icon appeared on the screen. My dad had left a voicemail? That was even more out of character than calling.

Now, I had a great dad. I just hadn't seen him since he retired to Florida. The Marines and then life got in the way.

I shook off the thought since there was no use getting myself worked up over nothing. My dad had probably just forgotten the time difference. It wouldn't be the first time, after all. Besides, I'd know in a second. I hit the play button and put my phone to my ear.

"Billy, is that you? No, of course not," my dad said as thunder boomed in the background. "Look, if I don't make it, trust me, it wasn't an accident... if you could come down here with a couple of those jarheads you called friends, well, that'd be just super." He paused, sucking in a deep breath and exhaling it into the receiver. "I'm going to try and — "

His words were cut off by the staccato crack of thunder. The phone must have slipped from his hand then because the next time my father spoke, his words were muffled and far off.

"You won't get away with this. My boy — "

"If your boy comes, your boy will die, you foolish old man," the voice said right before another crack of thunder split the air. Then the line went completely dead.

I stood there in shock. Had I just heard what I thought I'd heard?

No... surely not. There was no way. Could my dad be?

No...

I hit the call back button, causing the phone to go directly to voicemail again.

"Dad, this is Billy. What the hell is going on?" I barked, trying to keep the hysteria rising inside me from spilling into my voice. "Call me back."

As I ended the call, I turned and moved toward my closet. I threw the door open. Laying beneath a pile of clothing on the carpet was the lock box, and even though I didn't know what was going on, I grabbed it and

3

tossed it on the bed beside my old olive drab duffel. Then I started grabbing clothes, shoving them inside the sack.

Three minutes later, I was out the door and seated behind the wheel of my black 2007 Chevy Tahoe with my duffel on the seat next to me.

Normally, it took five days to drive to Florida from California, but I was going to do it in two.

CHAPTER 2

Forty hours later, I pulled the Tahoe in front of my dad's house. I was tired as all get out and hadn't showered in what felt like forever, but I didn't care. My dad still hadn't called me back despite me leaving so many voicemails, his mailbox had somehow gotten full. I wasn't even sure how that happened in this day and age, but it was what it was, I guess.

Trying to staunch the worry swirling in my gut, I hopped out of the Tahoe and approached my childhood home. It seemed so weird because I'd literally not seen the place in almost two decades, but it looked exactly like I'd remembered it what with the white picket fence and huge imposing gate.

Part of me wondered why my dad had moved back here after mom died, abandoning his place in Chicago for the sunny subdivision of my youth, but part of me knew. He'd wanted to hold onto her memory and being here helped him do that. I wasn't sure if that was actually healthy or not, but being that my dad was over seventy years old, I was inclined to let him do whatever he damned well pleased. Besides, it wasn't like he'd listen to me anyway.

No, my old man was stubborn as a mule.

As I approached the gate, I couldn't help but feel like something was wrong. I couldn't see into the yard because the honeysuckle was so overgrown, it blocked my view, but I still should have been able to see his truck. Hell, for all I knew, he kept his boat here too.

My dad's boat had been huge, and I would have been able to see it over the top of the gate if it was here. Man, I needed to get a grip. No matter what was going on, I had to keep my head.

Taking a deep breath, I turned back to the Tahoe and opened the door. Then I pulled the lockbox out from beneath the seat and input the combination.

A moment later, the lock opened. I pulled it free of the plastic case and tossed it on the seat. Then I unclipped the snaps holding the lid in place and flipped it open. My Glock 19 stared back at me. I hadn't even looked at the weapon since my last tour of duty, but it still looked as deadly as ever. There would have been days where I'd put seven hundred rounds through her for fun, but those days were long past.

As I pulled her free of the case, I instantly felt a little better. That said, I couldn't just carry her around in the open, so even though I didn't have a carry license in Florida, I dug out my inside the waist holster and hooked it to my leather belt just inside my pants. Then I checked the magazine in the Glock, ensuring all fifteen rounds were present and accounted for before shoving it into the holster and pulling my Tommy Bahama shirt down over it to hide it from view.

Sure, if I raised my arms, someone might see it, but hopefully, no one would make me do any burpees out here.

A grimace crossed my face as I stood up and shut the door to the Tahoe. Then I locked her even though I had nothing worth stealing. Hell, I was fairly certain people in Pleasantville still left their front doors unlocked. Still failing to plan was planning to fail. So I locked the door and shoved the dangle into my pocket.

Then I made my way toward my dad's place. The gate opened easily under my hand, making me think it'd been recently oiled because I remembered the gate always creaking like a son of a gun. Guess my dad had finally gotten to it after all these years. Mom would be so proud.

As the black, wrought-iron gate swung open, it revealed exactly what I'd known I'd see — nothing in the driveway. My dad's boat, a Catalina 36 Sailboat, was gone as was his black Nissan Titan, making me think he'd definitely brought it out on the docks.

A grimace flitted across my lips as I stared at the space the truck would have occupied. I never understood why my dad would go and buy a boat for over forty grand and then buy a Titan over an F150 because it was cheaper, but that was my dad.

Besides, the only thing my dad every used the Titan for was puttering around town or going to the dump. Heck, half the time I marveled that the Nissan could even carry enough to be worth taking to the dump.

"I wouldn't be standing here like an idiot if you'd answer the damned phone," I grumbled, glancing around the yard. Part of me wanted to go inside, but you didn't rush into a situation without doing surveillance first.

So I took a deep breath and tried to calm myself as I made my way along the walk past the azaleas. The door looked as it ever did. One of those solid white security doors hiding the carved oak front door. The windows were barred and shut, which had always struck me as odd when I was a kid, but they'd been there since my parents purchased the place. Besides, they did increase opsec, you know, in the event those traveling salesmen went for the hard sell.

"Hey, Dad! You there?" I called, rapping on the metal with my fist before pressing the doorbell with my thumb. It chimed loudly as I stood there, growing more anxious by the second.

I tried a few more times before pulling out my phone and calling for the gazillionth time. Again, there was no answer. As I stared at my phone, part of me wanted to listen to the message he'd left one more time, but I couldn't right now. It was time to get a move on.

Instead, I shoved the phone into my pocket and dug out my old Mickey Mouse key. That wasn't a joke. When I'd left home to fight for God and country, my mom had given me a house key stylized with Mickey Mouse because I'd loved the bugger as a kid. She said it'd keep me safe. It must have worked since I wasn't dead, yet.

I put the key into the lock and twisted as I pushed the memory aside so I could focus. As the door unlocked and I pulled it open, I tried the front door. It was locked too, but my key made short work of that.

Then I was inside. The first thing I noticed was the dust covering the shelves. It was a little strange since I remembered my parents being fairly clean. My dad must have neglected to dust all the knickknacks cluttering the shelves, most of which had belonged to my mom.

As I walked in past her collection of porcelain angels, I called out again. "Dad! Are you here? It's Billy." My voice echoed through the tiny house, but there was no response. A sigh escaped me. This wasn't good.

A quick glance around the place revealed dishes in the half-full dishwasher, but no other signs that someone had been here. Heck, even those seemed like they'd been there a while.

That's when a thought struck me. The last time I'd talked to my dad, he'd invited me out here to spend a few days on his boat, claiming we could stay on the old girl. I hadn't thought much about it at the time, and admittedly, I didn't know if it was even possible to "stay" on his boat, but maybe my dad was doing that?

I mean, it wasn't like he had to come back here for anything... but then why the weird phone call?

With that thought rattling around my head, I turned and made my way back toward the front door. Only as I approached it, I saw a huge mountain of a man standing on the porch. He was covered in tattoos and sported a bald head and a beard that fell to his mid-chest. He turned his cold gray eyes on me, seeming sort of surprised to see me.

"Who are you?" he asked like it made more sense for him to be here than me.

"Me? Who are you?" I snapped, my hand

inching toward my gun. If the guy saw me through the security door, he didn't seem to care.

The big guy shook his head at me. "I came to get something. Let me in." He smiled, revealing a mouthful of yellow teeth. "I promise not to break anything."

"Not gonna happen," I said, narrowing my eyes at him. Something about the guy bugged me, and while I didn't know what he was up to, I was way too high-strung to even think about trusting him. "You'll have to wait until my dad gets home."

His eyes widened at that. "Is that so?" he asked, and the glee in his voice stung me. It was almost like he knew something I didn't. "I suspect I'll be waiting a long time then." Those words sent a cold chill down my spine.

As I opened my mouth to ask him exactly what he meant, he waved off the comment.

"No matter. I'll come back later." He put two fingers to his temple and saluted me. Then he spun on his heel and walked away, leaving me standing there, barely resisting the urge to run outside and shake him down for information. I didn't, but it was a damned near thing, let me tell you.

CHAPTER 3

I was still standing there like a dumbass when I heard a car start moments before it peeled out and took off in a screech of burning rubber. While I couldn't see it because of the overgrowth along the gate, I found myself watching the street anyway.

Part of me knew I needed to get a move on and head to the docks to see if my dad, or at least his truck, was there. Only now I didn't want to leave. What would happen if I did? Would that jackass come back and rob the place?

I wasn't sure, but either way, I didn't have time to stand here and guard the place if I wanted to find my dad. So I put my big boy pants on and walked outside, making sure to lock the door behind myself. No point in making it easy to break in after all.

That done, I headed toward the street. Part of me wanted to lock the gate, but since it didn't normally lock, I didn't have many options. Damn.

I took a deep breath, trying to force down the anxiety gnawing away at my gut. Surely, if I headed to the docks, I'd find my dad busy cleaning fish or something. Right, not with that phone call.

What if I was too late?

No. I couldn't think like that. I had to do something, or I was going to go crazy. His phone went to voicemail again as I unlocked the Tahoe and slid behind the wheel.

A moment later, I was on my way toward the dock. While part of me had expected to be lost, the streets came back to me like I'd just been here yesterday. Even still, the differences were noticeable as I watched the houses on either side of the suburban street roll by. While most of the places I'd lived consisted of ticky-tacky houses, this neighborhood had been remodeled so many times over the years that most of the houses were nice looking.

I remembered my dad talking about it over the years. Every time someone passed away or moved to a new area, another owner would come in, knock the old place down to its frame and renovate. Guess that was what happened when the land was worth more than the house on it.

It still seemed a bit strange to me that people would actually want to live here what with the muggy weather, but I had to admit there was a natural charm to the state, and especially to a place like Pleasantville. It sang of crisp apple pie, and I dunno how else to say it, but the place reminded me of the Fourth of July block parties I always remembered as a kid.

Part of me wondered if they still had them, but judging by the way newly remodeled homes mixed with older houses, most of me was figuring they'd gone the way of the dodo.

Not that it mattered much. I was here for one reason. To find my dad. I knew, just knew, that the moment I found him, he was gonna laugh at me for being so worried. Then we'd knock back a couple Miller Lites and watch the ballgame.

I held that thought in my mind all the way until I reached the gate that led into the parking lot beside the docks. There was no line as I pulled into the ticketing booth, but there was an attendant. A guy about a decade younger than me with short curly hair and so many freckles, his face was more red than white.

"Howdy," he said as I approached. "It'll be ten dollars for the day pass." He held out his hand to me, and I smirked. Guess they didn't have automatic ticketing machines here.

"Sure," I said, pulling out my wallet and fishing out two crumpled fives. I handed them to him, and he presented me with a highlighter pink paper pass.

"Pleasure robbing you today," the guy said, smiling at me as he depressed a button, causing the mechanical arm blocking my way to lift with a wheeze of hydraulics.

I shook my head at the guy as I moved forward over those weird spikes that did irreparable tire damage when you went the wrong way. Soon as I was past, I spun the wheel and headed left around a bend in the road.

I found myself in the parking lot a moment later and much to my surprise, realized it was nearly empty despite the waterfront area teaming with shops. A quick glance at my watch told me why. It was barely 7 AM. Nothing was open. Of course, it was empty.

I drove around the parking lot anyway, my heart nearly beating its way through my chest with worry until I saw my dad's truck. His Nissan, complete with silly fuzzy dice hanging from the rearview mirror sat off to the left, practically hidden behind a big white Suburban.

Without pausing to think, I spun the wheel, angling across the parking lot for the truck. As I approached, I threw my own vehicle into park. My tires were on the lines, and I was cocked to the side, but I didn't care as I shut off the engine and leapt out of the Tahoe.

I was at my dad's truck in a flash. As I laid my hand on the hood, a chill ran through me. It was cold. The weather wasn't though, so that meant it'd been sitting here for a while, else it'd still be warm. A pang of fear shot through me, but I pushed it down as I walked around the car.

From what I could see, the inside of the truck looked pristine, and there was nothing in the bed, which I guess wasn't that strange. My dad was usually pretty clean, especially when it came to his toys. He was the type of guy who would have a week's worth of dirty dishes at his desk and then flip out if he got bird poop on his windshield.

I nodded to myself as I did one last pass. There was nothing odd about the vehicle. No signs of a struggle or anything. No, it more seemed like it'd just sat parked a few days, and since he had one of those permanent parking pass stickers in the corner of his windshield, I was guessing I'd been right. He must have taken the boat out and stayed on it for a while.

As I tried to make myself believe that, I headed toward the docks. I had no idea where my dad parked his boat though, so before I made it more than a few steps, I glanced back toward the dockyard entrance. I wasn't sure if that guy would know my dad, but since I didn't even know where the office was, it was as good a place to start as any.

I took a deep breath and then jogged toward the entrance. I made it about three steps before I resolved to get my ass on a Stairmaster for some cardio. I was a long way from doing ten miles hikes in full gear, that was for damned sure.

Still, I made it there quickly enough, and as I approached, the guy poked his head out to look at me. "Sorry, nothing's open." He had the decency to look sheepish as he looked me over. "I can give you a refund if you like. I'm not supposed to, but I'll make an exception." He shot me a congenial smile.

"No, that's okay." I waved him off. "I was wondering if you could direct me toward the office. I'm trying to find my dad's slip."

"The office is over yonder, but it won't open until nine," he replied, pointing one pale finger at a group of buildings to the left.

As I watched him do it, I was sort of amazed he wasn't burnt to a crisp. After all, I was pretty tanned, but the sun was still beating on my neck in a way that made me wish I had some sunscreen or a hat.

"Oh," I said, rubbing my chin. "Would you happen to know where Bob Ryder docks his boat?"

The guy stared at me for a moment, wheels turning in his mind. "Um... yeah, over on dock

J. Why?"

"What do you mean, why?" I asked before I could stop myself. "He's my dad, and I'm looking for him."

"Right, okay, sorry." He looked away, staring up at the blue sky like he was trying to discern the shapes of the wispy clouds overhead. "It's just that you're the second person this week who has asked where he docks his boat."

"I am?" I asked, trying to keep my sudden surge of concern from showing on my face. "Who else came by?"

"Big guy with tattoos. Said Bob was his dad." He stared at me hard. "Just like you did."

"He is my dad," I snapped, marching away from the booth and heading in the direction he'd pointed as quickly as I could without actually breaking into a run. My heart was starting to pound, but I sucked in a few breaths and forced myself to calm down.

Just because a tattooed guy had been here looking for my dad and had shown up at the house did not mean they were the same guy. Lots of people had tattoos now so it could be just a coincidence. Unfortunately, my military training didn't exactly lend me to believe in those.

As I approached the dock, I couldn't keep the sudden fear from exploding out of me. My dad's boat, the Storm Ryder, was there all right, but it was absolutely trashed. Even from here, I could tell someone had wrecked the thing, and as I'd said before, my dad kept his toys pristine.

I swallowed as I finally broke down and sprinted forward. My feet pounded on the wooden dock as I approached the dock. The wood by the boat was stained so dark, it was nearly black. The smell, like old fish, hit my nose, and as I glanced around for a bait cleaning station, my stomach clenched. There wasn't one anywhere near here, at least not one that would smell like fish left in the sun. Where was the stench coming from?

The boat stood in front of me, and as I hopped onto it, ignoring the fact my work boots would scuff the white surface and make my dad murder me, I headed down into its depths while trying to ignore the debris strewn about the cockpit.

Alarm bells went off in my brain, screaming at me that something was wrong as I moved further into the Catalina 36.

The lower level was worse. Pots and pans were strewn across the small galley, and the pillows and blankets had been flung on a heap beside the small bunks in the back. The small desk area was littered with old coffee stained charts and a litany of small tools that likely had been inside it at one time.

Had someone torn the thing apart looking for something? It seemed likely because even the pillows had been slashed open and the stuffing pulled out.

I swallowed hard, ignoring my sudden panic as I made my way through every nook and cranny of my father's boat, but he was nowhere to be found.

CHAPTER 4

"Hey, Max, it's Billy, is Vicky there?" I asked into my phone as I sat in the front seat of my Tahoe, nervously drumming the fingers of my left hand on the steering wheel. "I need a favor."

"Yeah, she's here," Max, one of my old buddies, replied. I had never been quite sure what he and his girlfriend did, other than cause trouble, but either way, both of them were good people to have at your back when the crap hit the fan.

"Good. Can I talk to her?" I asked, a thread of worry tingeing the edge of my words.

"Maybe..." His voice muffled on the other end of the line. "We're sort of busy at the moment. Is it important?"

"Yeah, my dad's gone missing," I said,

glancing over my shoulder toward where his boat was docked. I'd searched it literally ten times and had come up empty. I'd still not checked his truck, but it was next on the list. I just needed to go back to his house and grab the spare key. If I couldn't find one, well, I guess I'd have to jimmy the thing open. Either way, I wasn't getting into it now.

"Oh…" Max got quiet on the other end of the line for a moment. "You want me to come down there?"

"Not yet," I said, shaking my head even though I knew Max couldn't see it. "I just saw a guy, and I was hoping to get Vicky to do one of those character sketches she does."

"Are you playing CSI?" Max asked as the sound of his heavy footsteps echoed in the background. "Because I'm not sure you're smart enough for that."

"You're one to talk. You never met a problem you couldn't punch," I grumbled, my grip tightening around the phone. This was taking way too long, eating up time I didn't have. "Just put Vicky on the line. I'll owe you one."

"You owe me like six, already, but I'll put it on the list." He laughed in that horrible, "I own your soul" way he had. Then I could hear him talking to someone on his side of the line for a moment, but not well enough to make out what they were saying. "Here's Vicky."

"Thanks," I said, but I wasn't sure if he'd heard it because the next thing I heard was Vicky.

"What's up, Billy. Max says you need a drawing?" she asked in her high-pitched valley girl voice. It was weird because she was a short red-headed spitfire and too crazy to boot to own a voice like that. Still, I was glad Max had found her because he was the craziest son of a gun I knew.

"Yeah, I need a drawing. If I tell you what the guy looks like, can you draw him and send over the picture?" I asked, leaning my head back against the headrest in the Tahoe and staring at the gray ceiling.

"Sure. It'll take me a few minutes. Hang on a sec." The line got muffled as I heard her scrounging around. "I've only got a blue pen and some napkins. I can try again later when we get back home. Unless you want to wait?"

"Let's split the difference, and you do both?" I said, finally feeling like I was getting somewhere. I'd had exactly zero leads thus far, but I knew one thing. A tattooed guy had come looking for my dad twice, and if I found him, I'd make some headway.

"Okay, that's fine…" she mumbled before sighing loudly and launching into a string of questions. I never quite knew how she did it, or what the questions she asked meant, but at the end of it, she always came out with a near perfect sketch of the person. Sure, she wouldn't be able to show me the picture along the way to get my confirmation, but it was what it was.

"I think I'm done," Vicky said a few minutes later. "Let me text this over. If it's good, I'll work out a better drawing when I get home. I'll be honest, we're in the middle of something. It might be a while."

"Thanks, Vicky. I appreciate it." I shut my eyes, taking a deep breath. I was making progress. Not much, but some because now I had a picture. A picture I wouldn't need if I'd just shook that bozo down to begin with. "Send it over."

"Will do. Good luck, Billy. If you need us to come down there, you let Max know, okay? Don't be a hero." The concern in her voice surprised me, though I couldn't have told you why.

"I won't, Vicky. Promise. I'll catch you two later," I said as I hung up the phone, right as I realized I hadn't let her say goodbye.

A second later my phone dinged, indicating I had a text from Max. I opened it up and found myself staring at a pretty good rendition of Tattooed Guy, complete with all the tattoos I could remember drawn along the side. This was perfect. Anyone who had seen Tattooed Guy would immediately recognize him from the drawing. Now, I just had to find someone who had seen him. I knew just where to start.

I started the Tahoe. As music began to blare from the speakers, I instinctively turned it down. Then I headed back toward the exit.

Thankfully, the redhead was still there at the booth, and he waved at me as I approached. The barrier gate began to rise, but I ignored it and stopped beside his booth. He shot me a confused look as I rolled down my passenger window.

"Um... you need something?" he asked, looking at me. "Oh, yeah, you can re-enter with the pass for the rest of the day." He pointed at the paper I'd bought for ten bucks earlier. "Don't worry about that."

"Good to know," I replied, waving off the statement. "Just one more thing." I shifted the Tahoe into park and leaned close to the passenger side, holding out my phone. "Is this the guy you saw earlier?"

It took the guy a moment to realize what I was saying, and then his eyes darted from me to the phone. His smile practically slid off his face and shattered on the ground as he nodded. "Yeah. That's the guy."

"Have any idea where I might find him?" I asked, trying my best to look friendly. It was hard because he'd confirmed my suspicion that it was the same dude, so my insides were squirming like a worm bucket at a bait shop.

"No idea," he said as my grip tightened on the steering wheel. "Maybe try Malarkey's?"

He shrugged. "It's a bar where most of the locals hang out. Chances are good someone there will have seen him." He shot me a dopey, apologetic grin. "I'm too young to go myself..."

"Okay. Thank you," I said as fresh determination filled me. At least I had a plan. A bad one, maybe, but if it led me to my dad, that was good enough for me.

"Not a problem," he replied as I waved and rolled the window up. Then I used my phone to look up Malarkey's in Pleasantville, Florida.

A moment later, the directions were in my phone, and I was on my way.

CHAPTER 5

Malarkey's was just the sort of craphole I'd expected it to be, which probably says something about me. The outer walls had that bleached sandalwood look that had probably been nice twenty years ago but had long since fallen into disrepair. The neon green open sign was burning out, so the 'o' and 'e' were dark. The parking lot was cracked asphalt and filled with a bunch of Harleys and old pickups.

As I pulled the Tahoe into a lone spot in the corner and got out, I could already hear the country music blaring from inside. The ominous crash of guitar against a backdrop of crashing thunder set me on edge.

I slammed the door of the Tahoe shut, ran a hand through my short, close-cropped brown hair, and readied myself. I had no idea what

I'd find inside, but I knew it probably wouldn't make me happy.

The trip across the lot didn't take long, but I was surprised at the amount of broken glass littering the cracked asphalt. You'd think people would worry about that, but as I stepped up to the grimy black front door and pushed it open, I realized they probably didn't.

A chick who had probably been really pretty in high school but had since let a few years of hard living rough up her softer edges looked at me from behind the bar. Her scowl deepened as I stepped inside and surveyed the place.

Malarkey's was bigger than I expected and filled with pool tables, dart boards, and a few twenty-four-inch plasma screens displaying various sporting events. The jukebox in the corner was going absolutely crazy, throwing off neon flashes that danced across the ceiling. I turned my gaze to the patrons, searching for my dad.

A group of neo-Nazi looking skinheads looked up at me from the corner. They were dressed in matching stained wife-beaters, tattoos, and ripped up blue jeans and were way too busy with their beer and cards to pay me much mind.

Closer to the jukebox was a cowboy dressed in a white chamois shirt, a white Stetson, and a pair of wranglers. The girl standing beside him was all black hair, and even though I could only see the back of her head and her curves were covered by a yellow sundress, I could tell she was pretty.

Unfortunately, none of these people jumped out at me like they'd have any information, so I marched my happy ass over to the bar and sat down on one of the red vinyl upholstered stools. I leaned on the sticky sandalwood bar and glanced around one more time, trying to find a clue I'd missed before. There were none, and I was starting to think the guy at the docks had led me astray.

"Can I get you something?" the bartender asked in a voice that had smoked one too many cigarettes and chased it with one too many shots of cheap whiskey. She tried to smile, and I was surprised when it reached her eyes. It made her twice as pretty.

"Yeah, sure," I said, trying to think of a reason for my being here. Drinking would have worked, but I needed to keep my head on straight, and with the way things were going, if I started, I might not stop.

"Well…" she said after a moment of silence passed. "What will it be?" She gave me that, "please order something" look.

"Um… you have anything to eat?" I asked, my stomach rumbling. Two days of nearly no sleep and meals on the go hadn't kept me fueled, and now my body was starting to rebel.

"Got an early bird special. Two eggs over

easy. Biscuit and gravy. Hash browns." She gestured behind her toward a chalkboard with a bunch of stuff scribbled on it in nearly illegible print.

"That sounds great. Can I get that and some coffee?" I asked, fighting the urge to turn away and look around one more time. Maybe those skinheads knew something? They had tattoos after all. Only theirs looked a lot more like prison ink than Tattooed Guys had.

"Of course you can, sugar. I'll put on a fresh pot." She spun on her heel and disappeared into the back. I heard her muffled voice for a second, and then a minute later she reappeared, smacking her lips together like she'd just put on new lipstick.

As she came closer, I decided I didn't want to pick a fight with those guys just yet. Not when I still had some cards to play that were both easier and faster.

"Say, could you help me out with something?" I asked as the bartender set an empty mug and silverware on the bar in front of me.

"Oh, I'd love to help you out," she replied, leaning across the bar as she spoke and giving me a good view of her assets.

"I'm looking for a friend of mine," I said, ignoring her display as I pulled out my phone and showed her the picture of Tattooed Guy. "Know where I can find him? The guy at the dock said he might come around here?"

"Your friend, eh?" she asked, raising a shapely golden eyebrow at me. "Let me take a gander." She snatched the phone from my hand, and as she turned her eyes on it, the smile on her face evaporated, and her eyes hardened.

"What's wrong?" I asked as her jaw clenched.

She slid the phone back to me. "I'm really sure that isn't your friend." She looked away from me then, like she couldn't wait to be anywhere but here. "If that's who you're looking for, I'd suggest you just stop and head back to wherever it is you're from." She tried to smile, and this time, it didn't come anywhere near her eyes. "I'm serious. That fellow is nothing but trouble."

Her words were like a knife twisting in my gut. Dad was definitely in trouble. Not just small trouble either. I had to find him fast. If I didn't... no. I couldn't think like that.

"I appreciate the warning," I said as something behind her dinged, and she turned away to investigate. "But I'm trying to find my dad, and this guy keeps coming around..."

"Who is your dad?" she asked, turning and brandishing a glass coffee pot at me. Sloshing black liquid steamed inside, and as she poured it into my cup, she mumbled to herself. "Jesus, Darlene. You see a pretty face and your sense goes out the window."

"Bob Ryder," I said as I reached out to take my smoking hot cup. I blew on the steam before taking a sip. It hit my tongue like a burning fire, but in that good way diner coffee always seemed to. "He called me and asked me to come down, but he wasn't at his house."

"You try the docks?" she asked, quirking a smile at me as she returned the pot. "Wait…" She swallowed. "You mean that Tom was snooping around looking for Bob?" Her eyes filled with worry. "Oh no. What's that old fool…?"

"Tom?" I asked, putting my mug down and staring at her dead on. "Who is Tom?"

She fidgeted and looked away from me. "Tom Randolph is the guy from your drawing." She whipped one hand toward my phone, and I realized her fingernails had been chewed down to nubs. "He's part of the Scorpions."

"What are the Scorpions? Some kind of club or something?" I asked, my fingers practically white-knuckled as I squeezed the life out of my coffee mug.

"No." She shook her head. "The Scorpions are a gang in these parts. Rumor is they run drugs and whatnot, but the local cops haven't been able to do anything about it on account of the mayor being in their pocket." She sighed. "Old Bob didn't like it much. Said they weren't being good stewards of the town." Then, leaving her statement to hang in the air between us, she spun on her heel and headed into the back.

Her words sent a dagger of ice straight through my heart. My dad had gotten himself mixed up with a drug gang? Did that mean he was dead? No. I pushed that thought away even though the evidence was starting to mount. My dad might be bullheaded and crazy as the day is long, but he'd never let himself get killed. The old mule was way too stubborn to die.

I would find him, and if I had to beat my way through an entire gang to do it, I would.

"Um… so where can I find these Scorpions?" I asked when she returned with my breakfast and set it in front of me.

"Trust me, sugar. You don't want to find them." She let out a long, explosive exhalation of breath. "But I know your type. Like a dog with a bone. Won't stop till you got what you came for, even if what you came for is trouble plain and simple." Her fingers beat out a drum beat on the bar with one hand as she continued, "Look. The Scorpions will likely be on the east side of town. Down near Lawson's place. It's a bait shop, but I don't know how anyone drives a nice new BMW selling bait, if you know what I mean." With those words, she wiped her hands together. "And you'll not get another word out of me. No matter how cute you are."

"Thank you kindly," I said, turning toward my breakfast. I had half a mind to ignore my food and jet over to Lawson's right now to save time, but from the way my stomach was growling, I knew it needed fuel. Who knew when I'd get the chance again?

I grabbed my fork and started shoveling eggs into my mouth when the jukebox stopped. The sudden silence of it was so unnerving, I turned toward the music machine in time to see the cowboy backhand his girl across the face.

CHAPTER 6

I was on my feet and halfway across the room before she even hit the ground. Rage swelled up inside me, and my vision flared red around the edges.

"What do you think you're doing?" I snarled, my work boots beating a path across the stained floor of Malarkey's.

"Stay out of this, bud," the cowboy replied, glancing at me with a pair of beady, flat eyes. There was nothing in them but the cool, calm of a predator. Like a great white shark whose victims were women who couldn't protect themselves. I'd seen the type before. Dirt bags through and through.

"You're not supposed to hit a lady," I snapped, nearly to them now. That's when I realized how much makeup the brunette on

35

the floor was wearing. It was a thick mask I'd sometimes seen on battered women. Way too much concealer for there not to be something that needed it.

"I said, stay out of it," the guy said, turning toward me and squaring his shoulders like he was used to being the biggest, toughest guy in the room.

"No," I replied, taking a step closer to him, so there were only a couple feet between us. His hands started to clench and unclench as I stood there, staring at him dead on. This time I made eye contact with him. I found myself staring into an abyss of nothingness, confirming what I already knew. This guy had no soul.

"Do you know who I am?" the guy barked, and this time he took a step forward, so he loomed over me. He had me by half a head and a good fifty pounds, but that wasn't enough. Not nearly.

"Don't know. Don't care." I pointed at the woman on the ground, my finger practically shaking with rage. "You don't ever hit a lady. Didn't your mama raise you right?"

To her credit, the lady had pulled herself into a sitting position. As her eyes flitted over us, she scrunched backward, making an effort to look nearly invisible. Her face flashed with the knowledge that I was making things worse for her, a lot worse. Only as I stared at her face,

I realized I knew her. Or rather, I had known her. It felt like forever ago, but there was no way I'd have forgotten her face. Even with a few more lines etched into it.

Mary Ann Quinn. The girl I'd wanted to take to prom more than anything. The girl I'd skipped out on because I was getting deployed the week after. The girl I'd left to become this. It didn't make sense. The Mary Ann I knew was a firecracker. A spitfire ready to take on the world and make it run away screaming. If the Mary Ann I knew had gotten slapped, she'd have come up off that floor like a wild cat.

The cowboy stepped to the side, blocking my view of her as recognition lit her face. "Don't you mind what I do with my woman." He shoved his finger into my chest with enough force for me to feel it. "You need to shove off and mind your own business before my business gets to minding you. Understand, partner?"

"Oh, I understand," I deadpanned, grabbing his hand and twisting it as I shifted my hips, driving him face first into the dirty cement floor of Malarkey's. He crashed into it with the thwap of meat hitting a butcher's counter as I stepped through and locked his arm up behind him. "But here's what you don't understand." I applied some pressure to the hold, forcing his arm up until nearly the breaking point. "You don't ever hit a lady. You treat 'em with kindness and respect. You open car doors for them. But mostly? Mostly you thank the Lord above that a good woman would ever deign to look at you." I pushed on his arm, eliciting a whimper. "Are you following me, partner?"

"Y-yes," he cried through clenched teeth as he lay there, unable to do anything because I could pop his arm from its socket without even trying.

"Then apologize to the lady," I snarled, turning to look at Mary Ann. "Go on."

"I'm sorry," he wheezed through clenched teeth, but there was rage in those words. This guy wasn't sorry. Sorry that he'd gotten beat, sure, but that was all. What's worse, as his apology ripped out of his pig-headed throat, I knew what Mary Ann knew. This was going to get worse before it got better. Maybe a lot worse, and I wouldn't be the one paying for it. She would.

"Please just let him go, Billy," she said, her words a barely audible squeak. "Please…"

"You know him?" the guy on the ground snarled, and if he'd been mad before, he'd gone off the deep end now. He started to struggle, and this time, I let him go. He was on his feet in an instant, and before I could rightly process it, he flung a ham-sized fist at me.

I moved, years of training kicking in as I dodged the blow and lashed out with my own arm, catching him across the chest. The thud of impact rang up my arm as I stepped through the attack, throwing him off balance and knocking him to the ground. He crashed to the dirty floor once more, his head bouncing off the cement with enough force to make his eyes go glassy.

"See, here's the problem, friend. I can stop beating you up, but I think that just might make things worse for Mary Ann, here. That's not my intention." I took a step forward and knelt down with my knee across his throat, cutting off his air supply as I looked down at him. "What I'd intended was to make things better, and I was dumb enough to think I could stop your violence with mine. So here's what I'm going to do." I stood up, allowing him to breathe. He sucked in a gasp of air like he'd been about to pass out. As he rolled into a fetal position, I continued, "I'm going to let you walk out of here right now. I don't want to see you again. And if I hear about you going around Mary Ann again, I might just not be so amenable to seeing a fellow man change for the better. You understand, partner?"

I didn't wait for his reply as I turned on my heel and strode toward Mary Ann, offering her my hand. "Come on, let's get out of here."

She took my hand then, squeezing it with all the strength I remembered her having. A smile flitted across my lips, maybe all she needed was to be reminded she didn't deserve to get slapped around by a scumbag like that. Then again, what the hell did I know? I'd been gone for more time than I'd known her by a whole hell of a lot.

I reached into my pocket and pulled out two twenties. I slapped them on the bar on my way out and nodded to the woman behind it. "Sorry for the trouble."

The bartender gave me a long look before nodding back and pocketing the money. Satisfied, I turned and led Mary Ann outside and toward the Tahoe.

We were about halfway to my old beast when she dug in her heels and jerked her hand from mine like she was an oily eel.

"What do you think you're doing, Billy?" she cried, whirling on me like a sun devil. Tears filled the corners of her eyes before slipping out to run down her cheeks and ruin her makeup. "You can't just come back here after all these years and mess everything up." She turned back toward the bar, pointing at it with one shaking finger. "Chuck is a good man. He takes care of me—"

"He hits you, Mary Ann. He can't be a good man by any definition after something like that." I shook my head, wondering how I could possibly make her see that. It obvious to me, but somehow she was blind to that truth. "Come on, let me get you out of here, take you home."

"Arg! You don't understand," she cried in a rush of rage as she whirled on me, hands balled into fists. "You jackass..." She stopped then and buried her head in her hands. "I don't have anything..."

Then because I didn't know what else to do, I took a step closer and wrapped my arms around her, pulling her body against my own. She shuddered, crying into my chest, and as she did, I couldn't help feeling like I was somehow responsible. Sure, I knew that was ridiculous, that she'd made her own choices and whatnot, but I was also the one who had stepped into her business without being asked. That made me responsible. Didn't it?

CHAPTER 7

"So what's your big plan, Billy?" Mary Ann asked as she sat next to me in the Tahoe while I drove toward my dad's house. We were still pretty far from there, but I had nowhere else to go really. I couldn't just leave Mary Ann out on the street, nor did I want to risk going back to her place since it was likely Chuck would show up there. With that in mind, taking her to my dad's seemed like the best plan. Then I could go hunt down Tom and get my dad's spare key. Two birds, one stone.

"I'm taking you to Dad's. You can stay there for a bit while I take care of some things. Then I'll—"

"Are you being serious right now?" she snapped, interrupting me mid-thought. Instinctively, I turned toward her even though

I knew I should have kept my eyes on the damned road. That momentary glance was enough for me to see how angry she was. The old spitfire I'd remembered had returned... but where had it been all these years?

"Um... yes?" I replied, gripping the wheel tighter and focusing on the drive. There wasn't a lot of traffic, but that didn't mean there was no traffic. I could still rear-end someone if they came to a sudden stop, or worse, I could sideswipe a moving car. "I don't have a hotel or anything, and you said you couldn't go home..."

"So you think you can just walk back into town and play the hero? I haven't seen you since the night before prom." She harrumphed, turning away to stare out the window. "You know I waited for you, right? I sat there all night waiting. Thinking you'd show up, and then you never did..."

"I'm sorry, it's just —"

"No, you get to hear this. Then you can apologize afterward." She sighed and turned to look at me. I could feel her gaze hot on my face, begging me to look at her, but I couldn't do that and keep driving. "My friends told me I was crazy, that you'd shipped out already, but my Billy wouldn't have done that. He'd have said goodbye." Her voice cracked then. "He wouldn't make me go to his house all dressed up and alone on prom night to find out from his father he'd shipped out early. A real man wouldn't do that."

"I'm sorry," I said as the memory of the night flashed across my eyes despite my best efforts to stop it. I hadn't been a good man that night. "That's one of my biggest regrets. Everything happened so quickly... I tried to call, but the line was busy, and the next thing I knew I was on my way to boot camp. I got off and wanted to call, but then it was too late, and I thought maybe it was better. I wrote you a letter, a dozen letters, but I could never bring myself to send them..."

"Well, that and a few bucks will get you a bag of chips," she replied, glaring at me so hard, I actually pulled the Tahoe over so I could look at her. The car behind honked at me, but I ignored him as I slid to a stop in the parking lot of a convenience store advertising all manner of junk food in glowing neon script.

"I'm sorry," I said, turning toward her, and before I could stop myself, I'd grabbed both her hands. They were warm, soft, and comforting in a way I couldn't quite explain. "I really am..." I swallowed, shutting my eyes for a second as I collected my thoughts. "If you really wanna know, that was the reason I never came back. I knew I'd have to face you, and I was too much of a coward to do it."

I opened my eyes to find her staring at me with a look I couldn't discern across her face.

"You know," she said, taking a breath as she watched me carefully. "Chuck didn't start off so bad. He started off nice. Made me think of you, all stalwart and tough. No one could tell him what to do, and I thought he liked me. Hell, he didn't even hit me until we'd been together a couple years. He apologized so much, and I believed him. I know it sounds crazy, but after you, I thought maybe I deserved it. Because, you know, you just left me like that." She shook her head as her eyes began to fill with unspent tears. "Then before I knew it, I had no more friends, no one to talk to. It was just Chuck and me against the world, and if sometimes I messed up, well..." She touched her cheek then, and I could see the darkness barely concealed by the makeup. It damned near broke something inside me.

"You were the best thing that ever happened to me," I said before I could stop myself, and the next thing I knew, I'd wrapped my arms around her, pulling her into me. I buried my head in her neck, inhaling the scent of her, like fresh apple pie and springtime flowers. "And I was just a scared kid. Scared 'cause you made me want to be better, and then when I left I had this hole, and I guess, I just learned to live with it." I pulled away then, putting my hands on her shoulders as I stared into her eyes. "And now, I just feel so responsible."

"Now you feel responsible?" She laughed, shaking her head at me. "I'm a grown ass woman, Billy. Not some stupid kid. Sure, I might have gotten so mixed up I couldn't see up from down, but I spent the last twenty minutes trying to think of a way to explain to you why Chuck wasn't so bad, and you know what I realized? I couldn't think of one I'd believe if someone else was telling me. And that got me thinking that maybe you were right... so no, Billy. You're not responsible for me. I'm responsible for me."

"But if I'd come back sooner..." I mumbled, and as I spoke, she shook her head at me.

"But you didn't, and you can beat yourself over it, and baby, if you want to go ahead and do it, I'll let you because I'm still right pissed at you over prom, which is crazy because it was over twenty damned years ago, but no more than that. Everything else is my fault and Chuck's fault, and no one else's. His for being a horrible person, and mine for not seeing it." She inhaled sharply. "I can own that, so you man up and own what you did and stop making excuses."

"Okay," I said, watching her shed who she had been an hour before and rising above it like a newly reborn phoenix. In that moment, she was everything I remembered, and my heart ached because of it. "Let's leave the past in the past."

"Good," she said, pushing me away and crossing her arms over her chest. "So why are you back, Billy, 'cause Lord knows it isn't for me."

Her words snapped me back to the moment, back to what I'd come here for. To save my dad. As that realization hit me, quickly followed by the fact I had no time nor idea where to find my dad, and that the seconds on his life could be counting down as I sat here, I did the only thing I could. I pulled out my phone, went to my voicemail, and handed it to her.

"Listen to the message," I said as I keyed it up to start before turning my eyes back on the road. I waited for the big green Subaru Forester to lumber by before I jetted back into traffic, heading for my dad's place with renewed vigor.

Mary Ann put the phone to her ear, and as I heard my dad's muffled voice on the other end, a quick glance at her revealed her face paling. When it ended, she turned to look at me, and again I could feel her gaze on me.

"You need to call the police," she deadpanned. "I know you think you can take care of this," she waved the phone at me, "but you can't. Billy, this isn't a guy in a bar. This is the Scorpions. You couldn't fix everything then, and you can't now. Not by yourself." She shook her head at me, sending her raven locks fluttering around her face. "Are you listening to me?"

"He's my dad. I have to help him!" I said, determination steeling my voice. "If I don't, who will?"

"You don't know these people." She swallowed audibly. "They're killers... your dad is probably..."

"Don't even finish that statement," I replied, glancing at her as I took a hard left onto my dad's street. "I'm going to find him, and that's all there is to it."

CHAPTER 8

"Billy, even your dad told you to bring a couple friends with you," Mary Ann said as I went to the front door and pulled out my key to unlock it. "You didn't even do that."

"No, I didn't," I said, putting key to lock and letting myself inside. The place looked just as I'd left it, which was good. My muscles relaxed as I stepped inside and took a deep breath. I hadn't realized until this morning I'd sort of expected to find something nefarious going on inside.

"No. You just ran off all hot-headed to fix it." Mary Ann sighed, following me inside. "Just like you." Was that fondness in her voice? "Still, Billy, you need to go to the police and let them handle this."

"I will, but not before I look around. For all I

know, my dad's just gone off, and he'll come back and find I've gotten the police —"

"Do you hear yourself right now?" Mary Ann asked, marching around me and putting her hand on my wrist to stop me as I was about to pull out the drawer I remembered Dad using to store the keys when I was a kid. "You sound like me when I defend Chuck." She made eye contact with me, and it was like trying to stare down a hurricane. She took a step closer, putting one hand on my chest. "You may not be putting two and two together, but it's only because you're being a damned fool on purpose."

"Maybe," I said, pulling my hand away and jerking the drawer open at the same time. I was pissed because, at the heart of it, I knew she was right. Only, just because she was right, didn't mean it wasn't my responsibility. After all, my dad had called me, not the police. There was a reason for that. "But it's my choice to make. He's my dad and my responsibility."

Thankfully, the keys were there, and I hastily grabbed the keyring holding the spare for the Nissan. Then as I stared at the nearly empty drawer, I grabbed the other key and held it out toward Mary Ann.

"What are you doing?" she asked, eyeing the key carefully.

"That's the key to the house. I want you to stay put and safe while I go down to visit

Lawson's bait shop. I have a feeling it'll be just the place to catch what I'm after."

"Billy, listen to me. The only thing you'll catch is a beating if you go there." She squeezed my arm. "You might have some muscle, but try using the stuff between your ears. Do not go down there alone."

"Take the key," I said, pressing it into her hand and closing her fingers around it. Part of me expected her not to take it, but I couldn't have that. I didn't have time to watch over her and look for my dad. "I'll be back soon, and maybe we can get something to eat?"

"Are you hearing me?" she asked as I spun on my heel and headed toward the door. Truth was, I was hearing her, all too well.

But the thing was I might have to do some stuff I didn't like, and I couldn't do that with the cops around, nor with others who knew me. Worse, I didn't want someone else getting hurt on account of me.

"Yes," I said as I reached the door. "I hear you, and I'll be careful. If it looks bad, I'll leave. Okay?"

"You're lying to me, Billy Ryder." Her cheeks colored as her lips quirked into a thin smile. "I can tell on account of the way your nose scrunches up when you tell me. No, I know what you're thinking. You're trying to be responsible even though it's stupid." She let out a breath. "Fine. I'll stay here and twiddle my thumbs waiting for you, but I swear to God you'd better come back this time. If you leave me waiting all night…" Her words trailed off into nothingness as a lump formed in my throat.

"I'll come back," I said, and then I turned away because if I kept looking at her, I might just kiss her — not something I had time for now. I needed to find my dad. Distractions, even the good kind, were just that. Distractions.

"You'd better," she said as the security door swung shut behind me, and I found myself standing on the porch. The sound of the locks engaging filled my ears, and as I glanced behind me, the front door shut, hiding her from view.

It was for the best. If she was safe, I wouldn't worry about her.

That thought drove me as I got back behind the wheel of the Tahoe and made my way toward Lawson's while thanking my lucky stars for my phone because I'd have been hopelessly lost otherwise.

Lawson's wound up being in the middle of a strip mall filled with restaurants, nail places, and dry cleaners. None of those places seemed to be busy, let alone open, even though it was getting to be later in the day.

It smelled ten kinds of weird as I parked the Tahoe in a spot at the far end of the parking lot and got out. The Florida sun was blinding, but I ignored it as I moved toward Lawson's. A quick glance around the lot revealed only a couple other cars, none of which were particularly interesting or memorable.

Still, the sign in the bait shop's window said open, so I knew I hadn't wasted my time by driving here too early.

I made my way to the door and pushed it open. It jangled, signaling my entry into the shop, and I was immediately surprised at how big and small it was. It looked like a long hallway with doors that said staff only on one side. In between those doors were mostly bare shelves.

The other side was filled by a long glass case that displayed knives, lures, and assorted other gear. A few fishing rods hung on the wall behind it. Off in the corner was another rack with more gear, but that was pretty much it. I swung my gaze back toward the counter and spied another set of doors behind it. Why would they have so much space and not display their wares? Moreover, what could they possibly use such a large back room for?

"Looking to catch something?" a guy wearing a black tank-top, a backward ball cap, and blue jeans that revealed the top of his boxers said as he came through the door. He looked me up and down. "We've got a two for one special on worms." He pointed to a large fridge toward the door. It was wedged between a cooler with the word "ice" stenciled across it in big blue letters and a vending machine full of off-brand soda.

"Yeah," I said, moving up to the counter and looking into the glass. Everything in it looked like it might be okay quality, but all of it was priced way higher than it should have been. I wasn't sure if that was to gouge people or not, but I was willing to bet no one but the truly desperate bought any of this stuff, especially since there had to be bait shops closer to the docks.

"What are you after?" he asked, looking me over once more and settling a brittle smile on his face that made me think he didn't actually want to help me.

"Scorpions, mostly," I said, looking up at him. "Got anything to help me catch those?"

He stared at me for a long time before chuckling to himself. "Well, I'll be the first to admit you got some big old balls, so let me help you keep them." He leaned forward across the counter until we were only a few inches apart. "Just walk out the door before you find yourself in the middle of something you won't like."

I reached out and grabbed him by the back of the head and slammed him face first into the counter. His nose shattered in a spray of blood.

Much to my surprise, the counter didn't

break.

He cried out in pain, hands going to his face as I hauled him up a few inches. Blood gushed from his shredded lips, splattering across the counter as he tried to say something, but I stopped him by driving him back into a counter.

When I lifted his head again, there was a bloody smear where his face had been. He looked up at me with fear in his eyes.

"Look," I said, smacking the ball cap off his head. As it fluttered to the ground, I grabbed his hair and hauled him across the counter. "I just want to find my dad, Bob Ryder, and you're going to help me with that—"

A shotgun cocked, drawing my eyes toward it to find a tattooed punk with a nose ring the size of a baseball aiming a Mossberg at me.

CHAPTER 9

"I want you to think about something," I said as I released my grip on thug number one and turned to look at thug number two as he pointed his shotgun at me.

"What's that?" he asked, taking a step forward like he was going to shove me with the business end of the weapon.

"Think about how much it's going to hurt when I shove that gun up your ass." I took a step toward him, closing the distance between us.

"Are you high? I'm the one with the gun," he replied, narrowing his eyes as he pressed the weapon to my chest. "You best beg me not to kill you."

My hands whipped out, grabbing the barrel and wrenching it from his grip in a single movement. Before he could say a word, I had it turned on him and pointed at his stupid, confused face.

"What was that?" I asked, raising an eyebrow at him. "Something about which one of us had the gun and begging? I can't quite remember…"

"You're a dead man," he croaked, taking a step backward, and as he did, I shoved him with the barrel of the gun, hitting him hard in the solar plexus with the Mossberg.

"Really? Is that the best way to talk to the guy with the gun?" I replied as he crashed to the ground, grasping his chest in pain. "Here's how this is going to work. I'm going to ask where my dad is, and you're going to tell me."

"I don't know a goddamned thing about your dad," he snarled, and before he could say more, I shattered his nose with a quick strike from the butt of his weapon. He fell backward, sprawling the ground clutching his ruined face as blood poured from beneath his fingers.

"Wrong answer, dirt bag," I said, turning toward the guy I'd left on the counter. He was starting to rise, but stopped when I pointed the shotgun casually in his direction. "How about you, friend? Care to answer?"

"You're crazy if you think we'd tell you even if we knew." The thug spat out a gob of blood that dribbled down the counter but didn't make any movement toward me.

"You make an excellent point," I said, nodding and shooting him a congenial smile. "There's probably someone higher up than you two punks here, and I'd like to meet him." I whirled, smashing the toe of my work boot into the jaw of the thug behind me as he started to get up. His head snapped back, and his eyes went glassy as he collapsed back to the grimy floor unconscious. "Take me to the man in charge." I gestured for thug number one to move it.

"It's your funeral," the guy said, shaking his head at me like I'd done gone loco. Not that I gave a flying damn about what he thought. I had a mission, and that mission left no room for dealing with piss ants. "Boss is just through here."

I nodded, and the guy got slowly to his feet and moved toward a door behind him. I followed along as he pushed it open to reveal a long hallway that reminded me of those trailers full of offices I sometimes saw at job sites. I wasn't sure what was in those rooms because aside from the first room, an unoccupied office, the rest of the doors were closed.

The thug kept walking, heading toward the room at the far end. When he reached it, he turned toward me and gestured at it. "Mr. Ringo is through there—"

I cut off his words with a smack from the

shotgun, hitting him on the side of the chin and dropping him into an unmoving puddle. Then I kicked the door open.

My size thirteen shattered the particleboard jam, sending bits of wood flying through the air as the door whipped around so quickly, it hit the wall with a loud smack. Sitting there behind a desk was a pretty normal looking guy wearing a mustard-stained white button up and a loosened red tie.

He was balding and had bags under his eyes as he looked up at me through wire-rimmed glasses.

"Interesting," he said, unable to keep the weariness out of his voice. He looked me up and down before pushing his laptop closed and settling his hands on top of it. "Come in, have a seat." He gestured to one of the steel folding chairs in front of his desk.

Just seeing the smug bastard made me want to wring his neck until answers popped out. If he knew where my dad was, he was going to tell me. One way or another.

"Are you the man in charge?" I asked, taking a step forward into the room and bringing the shotgun to bear on him. None of the doors behind me had opened, which relieved me a little, but not enough for me to keep from checking my six every couple seconds.

"I am." He held his hand out toward me.

"Jack Ringo. At your service."

"Well, Mr. Ringo, I'm looking for my dad, and I'm told you're the guy to help me with that," I replied, ignoring his hand.

"Your dad?" The guy laughed, shaking his head as he dropped his hand back to the desk. "What would I possibly know about your dad?"

"I'm told your boys might have him," I replied, whipping out my phone and playing the message. Ringo listened, completely focused on it until it ended.

"I fail to see what that," he gestured at my phone, "has to do with me?" He drummed his fingers on the laptop. "I'm afraid you've just made a load of trouble for yourself for no—"

I cut off his words by bringing up the sketch of Tom on my phone and shoving it into his face. "This guy is one of yours, right?"

"Oh." His face dropped, and a sigh escaped his lips. "I see."

"So, I'm going to ask again. Where's my dad?" I said, and as I did, the guy leaned back in his chair.

"I really don't know Mr. Ryder's whereabouts." The way he said it shot my heart full of ice. Clearly, he knew enough about my dad and what had happened on the message to know my dad's last name. Maybe he knew a lot more. "And the man in your picture doesn't work for me." He shot me a thin-lipped smile. "He's much higher up than I am. You think they set up bigwigs in a bait shop? Hardly."

I wasn't sure if that was true or not, but I didn't care. Even if Tom didn't work for this guy, he probably knew something that could help. He would tell me that something.

"Who does Tom work for?" I asked, taking a thundering step forward.

"He works for Mr. Elliott," Ringo told me with no hesitation. "But I'm afraid that won't help you much."

"Call him," I replied, gesturing at him with the shotgun."

"I'm afraid I don't have Tom's number," Ringo said, shrugging. "Wish I could help — "

"Not Tom," I said, shaking my head. "Call Elliott."

"It's really a bad idea. Look, you walk out of here, and I'll forget this all happened. You go back and do whatever it is you do. Ride around in a convertible, bang some strippers, whatever." He made a shooing motion. "But if I call Elliott, things are going to get bad for you."

"I am not going to repeat myself," I said, letting the emotion drain from my voice.

"Fine, but don't say I didn't warn you." With that, Ringo moved toward the black phone on his desk, hit the speaker button, and then a speed dial button. It rang for a few seconds before a female voice answered.

"Hello, you have reached the office of James Elliott. How may I help you?"

"Hey, Nancy. I got a guy here with a shotgun pointed at me who says he wants to talk to James. I'd be much obliged if you could see if he's got a minute."

"Understood. I think he's in a meeting, but I'll see if he can break away for a minute." The line got quiet as Ringo turned to look at me. The whole thing struck me as incredibly businesslike, making me think there was a lot of money involved. If that was true, these thugs were nothing compared to what I'd find if I kept digging. Not that it mattered. I was going to find my dad, even if I had to beat my way to the penthouse suite.

"Well, you done really screwed the pooch now," Ringo said, shaking his head at me. "And it was fixing to be such a nice day. Word of advice. Make sure your will and whatnot is in order."

Before I could reply, the voice of a gruff, older-sounding man came on the line. "Jack? What's this about a man with a gun?"

"There's a man here, Bob Ryder's boy. Says he's looking for his dad, and if you don't help him, he's going to kill me," Ringo replied, shrugging at me.

"I'm afraid, I'm not going to be able to help him," Elliott said.

"What do you mean you can't help?" I snarled, taking a step forward and glaring at the phone even though I knew the guy on the other end couldn't see my face. "Why the hell is that?"

"Look, son. I'm not in the business of helping people, especially when doing so involves helping someone find someone else I went to great pains to get rid of." There was a pause. "But I'll tell you what I'm going to do. I'll arrange for you to meet him real soon in the next life, okay?"

"I'm serious. If you don't tell me where he is, I'm really going to shoot your friend here," I said, turning my eyes to Ringo. Anger and frustration flared inside me. These guys weren't taking me seriously. I fixed my eyes on Ringo. "Tell him."

"He does seem serious," Ringo said in a bored tone.

"Look, son, we both know you're not —"

I fired the shotgun, blasting Jack Ringo full of buckshot and sending his bloody body hurtling back against the wall. He hit with a wet thud before crashing to the floor, leaving a bloody smear on the wall.

"What was that?" Elliott cried, suddenly alarmed. The sound of it pleased me. They'd take me seriously now. "Jack, are you okay?"

"Jack is not okay, and if you don't help me, neither will you be? Understand?" I asked as I crossed the room and dug Jack's cell phone after his pocket. Then I shoved it into my own pocket and scooped up the laptop from the desk, slinging it under my arm.

"Oh, I understand. We'll be in touch." The line went dead, leaving me standing there with the sound of the shotgun ringing in my ears.

CHAPTER 10

I sat behind the wheel of my Tahoe and stared out the windshield, trying to will my heart to stop pounding. Adrenaline was still surging through me, causing me to shake as I gripped the wheel. I'd just killed a man, and what's more, I'd done it in cold blood.

Worse, I had no leads. The two yahoos I'd taken on inside the place had been gone by the time I'd come back out. The only things I'd gotten out of it were Ringo's phone and computer, but I wasn't going to be able to hack into them or anything. I'd need an expert for that, and I knew just the guy.

First things first, though. I had to check out my dad's truck. If it had a clue, maybe I wouldn't need to hack anything.

I took another deep breath and started the

Tahoe. She roared to life as AC/DC's Highway to Hell came blaring across the speakers like it was giving me a sign. I bristled slightly and nodded. I just wanted to find my dad, but what was that saying about the road to hell being paved with the best of intentions?

The drive to the dock was a blur, but when I got there, I was surprised to see how crowded it'd become. As I waited in line to get back inside, I practically strangled my steering wheel. If the truck turned up no clues, I had no idea what I'd do.

Guess, I'd cross that bridge in a minute. No use thinking about it now.

The redhead was still in the ticket box, and as I approached, he waved at me and opened the gate. Guess I was memorable.

I followed the path through the lot until I reached my dad's Nissan. It was no longer the only car in the lot because numerous cars were parked all around. Not enough to keep me from parking close by, though.

As I shifted the Tahoe into park and jumped out, the cool, salty sea breeze hit me. I sucked in a breath, allowing the taste and smell of it to carry me back to when I was a kid fishing with my dad. We hadn't had our own boat then, but that hadn't stopped my dad from bumming trips from his friends or if it was a real special occasion, booking us on a fishing boat.

Jesus, I had to find him. If I didn't, I'd have

no one left. My hands curled into fists as I approached the Nissan. They'd better not have killed my dad because if I couldn't rescue him, I'd damned sure avenge him. The Scorpions would not like that one bit.

I reached into my pocket, willing myself not to think about that, and pulled out the key fob. I hit the unlock button.

The truck exploded into a fireball of doom that sent me flying backward through the air. I hit the ground hard on my back, skidding across the asphalt as debris pelted me. Pain shot through my back, legs, and chest as heat washed over me, singeing my eyebrows and burning away my arm hair.

As I lay there, my brain filled with fog. Instinctively, I curled away from the flame, tucking myself into a ball. It was the only thing that saved me because as I rolled to the left and balled my body up, a bullet ricocheted off the asphalt where my head had just been.

The sound of it sent my body into action. Years of training took over. I rolled more, instinctively taking cover beneath a battered, blue Honda Accord. Another bullet popped the Honda's tire as I lay there gasping for breath.

Someone had put a bomb in my dad's car, and what's more, now they had started shooting at me.

How could I be so damned stupid? What if

they'd taken a pot shot at me before when I'd been wandering around here like a dumbass? Worse, what if I'd tried to open the Nissan's door and blown myself up?

As those unhelpful thoughts filled my brain, another one hit me. They'd put a bomb in my dad's truck. They'd been trying to kill him, and that meant the guy on the phone... No. I couldn't think that way. I had to get out of here and find him. I couldn't wallow. Not with the Nissan still burning and some jackass shooting at me.

Sirens echoed in the background, but I willed myself to focus, to allow the world around me to come into view as another bullet struck the asphalt in front of the Honda before ricocheting into the undercarriage only inches from me.

"What did you think was going to happen," I muttered to myself as I rolled out from under the car, careful to keep it between me and where I thought the shooter might be. "Did you think you were just going to go and kick a hornet's nest and not get a few trying to sting you?"

A bullet flew over the hood of the vehicle as I crouched down, hitting the parking lot just behind me. The sirens were closer now, but that was fine because I'd seen the muzzle flash from a building closer to the dock. It was a taller one belonging to a restaurant that boasted ten different ways to fry fish.

I ducked down, reaching behind my back and grabbing my Glock from the holster. Then I leaned close to the Honda and held my breath for a second. I exhaled while throwing myself to the side. I brought my gun up as a bullet zinged by me and fired three quick shots in the direction of the shooter. This time I saw movement, presumably the sniper dropping to avoid my fire.

"Good," I mumbled as I hit the ground hard, a stab of pain slicing through my shoulder as I rolled to my feet and sprinted forward, careful to keep cars between me and the shooter. He rose a few times, but a shot made him duck back down.

My chest heaved, and my lungs burned by the time I made it to the restaurant. Thankfully, there was no one inside, nor had my shots attracted any attention. Then again, there had just been a car explosion. Maybe people were too focused on that to hear my shots?

I wasn't sure, but either way, I didn't want to get caught with a gun out. I shoved it back into my holster as I pushed through the door. The hostess, a girl in her mid-twenties with glossy pink lipstick spied me as I came in, and as she opened her mouth to speak to me, I waved her off.

"Sorry, my car just backfired, got a phone I can use?" I asked as I eyed the place.

"Um… I just called 911, are you okay?" she asked in a cutesy voice as I found the stairs and started toward them.

"Yeah, just a little banged up. Mind if I use the restroom? Wanna wash the blood off," I said, not bothering to wait for a response as I ran up the stairs. I reached the second floor and looked around, but found no one there.

I took a few steps forward, heading toward the balcony area where I'd seen the shooter, and as I did, I felt a garrote slip around my neck.

CHAPTER 11

My hand just barely came up in time to keep the garrote from slicing into my carotid artery. As my flesh tore open and blood spilled down my hand, I threw myself backward with my legs as hard as I could.

We slammed into the wall behind me, and the wire around my neck loosened enough for me to suck in a breath. Before I could pull the garrote free with my bleeding hand, it cinched down again. Agony ripped through me as I tried to regain my footing. My feet scrabbled across the tile as the wire cinched tighter, spilling more blood down my hand. I could feel the cold kiss of the garrote against my neck, biting into the flesh, and I knew that soon, it wouldn't matter if I had my hand in the way.

My vision started to dim as I threw my head backward, trying desperately to find purchase in the face of my attacker. It must have worked because I felt my skull impact something squishy and crunchy.

The garrote loosened enough for me to breathe. I sucked in a lungful of air that burned all the way down as I whirled, bringing my left leg up. As I faced my opponent, my heel snapped down, catching her in the knee with a solid kick. Her leg bent sideways with a horrific snap, and she crashed to the ground, one gloved hand gripping around the garrote.

Her face scrunched up in pain as she bit down a cry and tried to regain her focus. Blood gushed from her busted lips, spilling down her chin and staining the waitress uniform she'd been wearing.

"Now, hold on a minute," I said as her dense, hard packed muscle coiled like a snake about to spring, and a knife slid from beneath her sleeve and into her hand. "Let's just talk a minute."

The weapon flashed at me as I jumped back a step, narrowly avoiding the blade.

"There is no waiting for you. Only dying!" she snarled, rearing back like she was going to throw her knife at me. Before she could, my boot lashed out, catching her in the chin. Her jaw snapped together with a crack as she sprawled backward. Her head rebounded off the cheap linoleum, and her eyes went distant and far off. The knife slipped from her hand and clattered to the ground.

Thankfully, no one had shown up yet, but since I could hear sirens right outside, I knew it wouldn't be long. All it'd take was for one of the cops to ask the hostess I'd seen on my way in about the explosion.

"Just stop," I said, kicking her knife away. I knelt across her chest and pinning her to the ground with my knee. "I don't want to kill you."

The assassin didn't respond because she was still dazed, so I took advantage of the situation and rolled her over onto her belly and frisked her. I found a pistol, a nice compact CZ 75, which I relieved her. Part of me wished I'd found something to tie her up with, but being that I was fairly sure I'd dislocated her left knee, I didn't much see the point. Besides, as I pinned her wrists behind her back, she started to struggle like an oiled pig.

"Stop," I said, as she thrashed, but when she didn't, I grabbed a handful of blonde hair with one hand and hauled her head backward a few inches. "If you don't, I will slam you face first into the floor until you do."

She stopped, which was good because I could hear talking down below.

"Who sent you?" I asked, knowing I didn't have much more time.

"I'm not telling you anything," she spat. No. There was definitely no time for this.

I hauled her up onto her feet, causing her to cry out in pain. She stumbled as I dragged her outside toward the balcony and shoved her against the edge.

"Look, you can tell me what I want to know or you can take the long trip down," I snapped.

Her lips curled into a bloody, self-satisfied smile. "You'll do it won't you?" She punctuated the words by hocking a bloody loogy onto my chest. "Well, go on then." She wobbled backward, pulling out of my grasp as she forced herself up onto the edge. "Or do I have to help you?"

I reached out, grabbing her by the throat. As I pulled her forward, I heard people coming up the stairs. Damn. No more time. I threw her to the ground and sprinted for the service door to my left. I'd barely darted through when I heard the cops enter the room and look around.

To her credit, the lady didn't resist them, and from my position, I could see them haul her off, which didn't surprise me what with the pistol and the giant ass sniper rifle inside. They might have found me, but since she was anything but cooperative, I was left all to my lonesome. At least for the moment.

Sure they'd be back, I made my way toward the restroom so I could pretend like I'd really been inside this whole time, but before I made it, I heard the squeal of burning rubber. My head darted toward the balcony in time to see a black SUV roll down its windows and fill the front of the restaurant with automatic weapons fire. I rushed forward, about ready to pull my Glock and fire back when the SUV hit the gas and took off toward the exit. It hit the wooden safety arm and tore it free in a spray of wood and fragments before peeling out into the road and taking off.

Below me, the girl I'd just fought lay dead in a pool of her own blood, but what surprised the hell out of me was that the cops next to her weren't even hit. No, the person in that vehicle had managed just to take out the assassin and no one else. With an automatic weapon, no less.

I swallowed hard. That was a professional hit, and while I wasn't sure if the hitter had been working with the sniper, clearly someone hadn't wanted her talking.

I turned my gaze back toward the exit as cops leapt back in their cars and took off after the SUV. Thankful for the distraction, I made my way downstairs. There was so much commotion that no one gave me more than a passing glance as I made my way outside and headed toward the Tahoe. I needed to get out of here before this place became a three-ring circus. If that happened, I'd be stuck here all day, and I didn't have time for that.

Instead, I got into my Tahoe, tried to ignore how hurt I felt, and opened a bottle of water. I gulped it down and wiped my mouth with the back of one hand before tossing the empty bottle on the passenger seat floor. Then I looked over at the laptop sitting on it.

"Screw it," I said as I started the Tahoe and began making my way out. I couldn't go through the normal exit what with the cops, so I drove to the side entrance that read members only. I was ready to make an excuse, but as I approached, I found they were already routing everyone through that exit because of the damage to the barrier.

I pulled up my contacts list, scrolled a minute, and hit call as I followed the few cars ahead of me out the gate and away. The sound of it ringing came over my Bluetooth, and as it reached the fourth ring, someone picked up.

"Hullo?" came the tired voice on the other end, followed by lips smacking in the way that told me I'd just woken him up.

"Hey, Ren. It's me, Billy. I need a favor, but I think you'll like this one," I said, turning onto the road and heading back to my dad's place. My back hurt like a son of a gun, and I needed to wash off the blood and change my clothes.

"Billy? Why are you calling so early?" he muttered, and I heard him moving around. "It's not even noon."

"Sorry," I grumbled. Ren didn't quite keep normal hours, but I didn't have time to call later in the day. I needed his help now.

"So what's this favor?" he asked, curiosity starting to leak through his tiredness.

"I've got a laptop that belongs to a drug runner, and I need to know about a guy named Elliott. Got a phone too. Help me get what I'm after, and everything else is yours. I'll even throw in a case of Corona." I took a deep breath. I had nothing I could really offer Ren, but I needed his help. Hopefully, that would be enough.

There was a long pause that almost made me think I'd been disconnected, only the screen on the console of the Tahoe told me otherwise.

"Okay," he replied with the barest edge of excitement in his voice. "Where are you?"

"Pleasantville, Florida," I said, breathing out a sigh of relief that he'd agreed to help me. I wasn't sure exactly what Ren would do with the information he found on the laptop, but I was fairly sure it'd be profitable. Why? Because while his house may have cost a hundred grand, the inside of the place was so lavish it had to have cost twenty times that.

"Oh, that's not too bad. I'm in Orlando. I'll be there in a few hours." He paused. "Am I going to get shot at?"

I glanced back at the docks. "Probably."

"Okay, I'll pack a vest then."

CHAPTER 12

By the time I pulled up in front of my dad's place, I was clenching my teeth in an effort to ignore the agony my body had become. The adrenaline that had numbed my pain had long since faded away, leaving me feeling like a ragged wound. Cuts, bruises, and everything in-between screamed at me as I shifted into park and practically fell out of the Tahoe and onto the pavement.

After what felt like forever, but wasn't more than a few seconds, I pulled myself to my feet, grabbed my duffel from the back seat, and made my way to the house. My back felt like a nest of fire ants had assaulted me, and my neck hurt like a son of a gun.

My legs were shaking by the time I mounted the porch and fell against the door. I thought about trying to unlock it, but as I dropped my duffel to the ground with a heavy thwap, I really wasn't sure I could do it because my hands were shaking too much.

I pressed my thumb against the doorbell and waited, my forehead pressed against the wall because it was cool, and I was so damned hot.

"Who is it?" I heard Mary Ann ask, and as I turned my head back toward the door, I saw her peek at me from between the blinds of the small window beside the door. Her eyes went wide, and the next thing I knew, the door was open, and she was out on the porch with me.

"Jesus, Billy. What the hell happened to you?" she asked, her voice filled with near panic.

"Someone blew up Dad's truck," I replied. "I wasn't in it, but I wasn't exactly far away either."

"What?" Mary Ann cried as she hustled me inside. "I don't understand."

"Someone blew up the truck. There was a bomb in it, and when I went to unlock it, boom," I muttered, trying to swallow a sudden pang of agony as she threw my arm over her shoulder and led me to the couch. I barely made it to there before I collapsed.

"Oh my God, your back looks like hamburger," she squeaked as I lay there flopped across the cheap old leather sofa like a useless sack while she went back to the door, pulled my duffel inside, and closed it. Then she locked it for good measure.

"We need to get this cleaned up, and then you need to rest." She shook her head. "What you really need is a doctor, but I know you're too stubborn for that." She bit her lip, chewing on it for a moment before nodding resolutely. Then she grabbed my arm and tried to haul me to my feet.

"Ow!" I cried, shifting so I could let her pull me to my feet while not also yanking my arm from the socket. "That hurts."

"I don't want to hear it, Billy Ryder. I'm done coddling you for being stupid. Now you can man up and face the consequences." She glared at me, and I suddenly felt like a little kid getting admonished by his mother.

"Yes, ma'am," I said, looking at my feet as she led me from the couch toward the bathroom.

"Strip," she demanded, moving past me into the tiny space and turning on the shower. I stood there like a dumbass as she turned it on and held her hand out under the spray, waiting for the temperature to adjust. When she was satisfied, she turned back toward me.

"Why are you still clothed?" she snapped, marching toward me. She grabbed the hem of my bloody shirt and jerked it up over my head. My soul screamed in sheer, gut twisting agony, and I nearly collapsed to my knees. Hell, I would have if she hadn't caught me, wrapping her arms around my waist and steadying me. Even still, it was a near thing, and we both almost wound up on the cold tile floor.

"Sorry," I muttered as she steadied herself.

"Welcome," she said before she sat my ass down on the toilet. Then she jerked my boots off and flung them to the ground. A second later, she wrestled my bloody jeans off and tossed them alongside my boots and socks.

"You can keep your boxers on." She wrinkled her nose at me. "The puppies are cute though." With that, she shoved me into the shower.

I screamed like a little girl as the boiling hot water hit my ruined back. Crimson swirled around the drain in the floor as I leaned heavily against the wall, my legs shaking from the effort of holding myself upright.

"Turn around," Mary Ann commanded as she reached into the spray and ran her hand over my back. It hurt, but as she picked out bits of rock and glass, I realized I was starting to feel a lot better.

It felt like forever, but eventually, the water stopped running red, and as Mary Ann shut the tap off and pulled me out, I realized she was standing there in her bra and panties. Her clothing had been neatly folded and placed beside the sink. I hadn't even seen her strip her clothes off.

"Dry off while I find a first-aid kit," she said, wrapping a towel around herself before handing me one. Then she knelt down and pulled open the cabinet beneath the sink. A second later, she was on her feet with a first-aid kit in her hand.

"I'm almost surprised he has one of those," I said, my own towel now around my waist. "I half-expected you to pop up with rubbing alcohol or peroxide."

"Oh, those are down there, but they'll actually do more damage than help. Good old soap and water should be fine for you."

She shot me a smile and stepped into the hallway, motioning for me to follow her out of the room when the sound of gunfire filled my ears.

CHAPTER 13

Without thinking, I threw myself forward, grabbing hold of Mary Ann and dragging her to the floor as gunfire tore through the front wall of my dad's house, shattering the windows and perforating the front door.

All pain forgotten, I tried to shield Mary Ann with my own body as all hell broke loose outside. As I lay there, the whole world coming around me and ricochets filling my ears, I grabbed Mary Ann and jerked her backward into the bathroom. So far, it remained relatively safe thanks to the couple walls between us and the front room, but I knew that wouldn't be enough.

"Get in the tub," I said, trying to be heard over the din as I grabbed my Glock from where it lay next to my pants and checked to make sure it was ready to go. She hadn't moved by the time I was satisfied by the weapon, probably too shocked by all the shooting.

I could believe that though. While I'd spent enough time in combat to keep myself from freezing, I remembered my first time like it was yesterday, that paralyzing fear that fills you and lets you know you could very well die. The key to not dying though? Moving past that.

"I said get in the tub," I hollered, trying to be heard over the din as I grabbed her arm and yanked her toward the still wet tub where I'd taken my shower. She looked at me, eyes far off and scared, and because I didn't have time to argue with her, I forced her toward the tub. "Stay down. I'll take care of this."

"How?" she asked, snapping back to reality and fixing her perfect eyes on my face. Worry swam through them, and her lip trembled, but that was okay because I wasn't going to let anything happen to her. I'd brought her into this situation, and I'd damned well get her out.

"I'm going to kill them," I said as the gunfire stopped. The silence of it after so much racket was eerie. "Going to keep you safe."

As I spoke, she moved into the tub and crouched down. "Billy..." She gestured at the gun in my hands.

"I don't want a lecture right now, ma'am," I said, nodding to her. "I'm of a mind that only

God gets to judge us, so I'm just going to arrange the meeting." She smiled at that, but I was already turning away and pushing her from my thoughts.

It was silent which meant they were waiting. I crouched down as I peered back into the hallway, but the door was still intact. Sure, it had a few more holes in it that let the sunshine through, but otherwise, it was still barring the entry. Good, maybe no one was inside.

I crept forward, gun at the ready. A head poked up past the window, and as the thug tried to look inside, I fired my Glock. The bullet caught him just above the left eyebrow, blowing a skull-sized hole in his head.

As he collapsed out of sight in a spray of blood and gore, more gunfire erupted from outside. I dropped flat on my belly, thankful I was still mostly shielded by the hallway. Bullets tore through the window and door, pelting the furniture in the living room and spraying the insides of the couch across the floor.

I focused, trying to divine the angle of attack from the impacts, but it was no use. There were way too many shots and ricochets for me to tell.

Instead of firing blindly and giving away my position, I began to make my way to the left, hoping I could get to the back door and make my way around to flank them. It might mean leaving Mary Ann alone for a bit, but it was my best chance because anyone willing to stay here and keep shooting wouldn't think much of setting the place on fire and smoking us out.

"I should have never come back here," I chided myself as I crawled forward on my elbows. "Of course the Scorpions would come here." I shook my head in anger as I moved into the dining room. It was a small room attached to the kitchen and led into either the garage or the sunroom depending on which door you took.

As I got into a crouch and began to edge toward the sunroom so I could reach the back door, the garage door blew inward in a spray of wood. I fired, putting two rounds in the intruder's chest and face without thinking. He collapsed backward into his pal, stunning him so he couldn't shoot me with the shotgun in his hands.

I didn't have that problem, so I shot him too. His life evaporated in a spray of crimson mist as he collapsed backward into a heap on the floor. The gunfire outside ratcheted up a notch, but I ignored it as I surveyed the scene. It didn't take a genius to figure out what had happened. These guys had come through the garage. It made me realize how dumb it was to have a security door on the back door and the front door, but not the one that led from the garage to the house.

Filing that thought away for later, I edged forward, glancing into the garage. Fortunately, I saw no one else. I bent down and scooped up the Remington 870 Express Tactical the second thug had dropped. All seven rounds were still in it. Good.

Just as I'd thought, the man door on the other end of the garage had been kicked in. Thankfully the garage door itself was still down. There were a few errant bullet holes in it, but nothing much. There was, however, my dad's old yellow Mustang. He'd been working on it for years, and while it ran, it was far from restored. A smirk crossed my lips as I moved toward it and pulled open the door. Then I reached under the seat and pulled out the key hidden there.

I put it in the ignition, causing it to roar to life. As its engines rumbled, gunfire erupted from outside. Bullets blasted through the garage door, spraying debris across the floor, but I ignored it. I threw the car in reverse and wedged the shotgun down on the gas pedal. The Mustang took off in a squeal of tortured rubber as I launched myself from the car. It crashed backward through the garage door, and as it did, everyone outside focused fire on it.

I wasn't so easily distracted. I took down the

three thugs standing on the driveway while they were still focused on the Mustang. As their lifeless bodies hit the cement, the Mustang hit the gate, tearing it free in a shriek of tortured steel and revealing a black SUV remarkably similar to the one I'd seen at the docks. A long-haired guy smoking a cigarette leaned out the driver's window.

We made eye contact the split second before the Mustang plowed into the side of the vehicle, rocking it sideways into the street. A quick look around revealed no more attackers in front of the house, so I sprinted across the clearing while the driver hit the gas. The SUV squealed in pain, pinned by the Mustang as I raised my gun and fired a couple quick shots into the tires.

They blew out, and the spinning wheels hit the ground, tearing the tires to shreds as the SUV started to lurch forward on its rims. Sparks shot from them as the SUV began to tear away from the Mustang.

I sprinted across the driveway as the driver grabbed for something on the seat next to him. He raised a Colt Python at me, and I gave him the meeting he'd always wanted with Saint Peter outside the pearly gates.

I stood there for a moment, chest heaving before moving forward. I tore the shotgun from the Mustang, causing it sputter and stop like a dying beast of war. Then I turned to check the SUV. Only before I'd even pulled the door open, Mary Ann's scream from inside the house shattered my concentration.

CHAPTER 14

As I spun back toward the house, gunfire erupted behind me. I threw myself to the side as bullets chewed up the front lawn, turning my dad's pristine summer sod into so much torn up dirt. I rolled as the line of bullets tore an erratic path behind me. I came up in a roll and fired at the attacker.

My shots missed, but they were enough to make the guy beside the SUV duck behind it for cover. Damn. There must have been another one inside. How could I have been so careless?

Thankful for my second chance at life, I scrambled to my feet and charged forward, emptying my Glock in an effort to keep the son of a gun pinned down.

Thankfully, he didn't decide to take one for

the team and pop out to shoot me, and a second later, I was at the SUV. My Glock empty, I decided to use it as an improvised club as I put one foot on the hood of the smoking Mustang and vaulted over the hood of the SUV.

I came down on the thug just as he was peeking out to pump me full of holes. My Glock crashed into his rising shoulder with a loud crack.

He screamed in pain as I landed on top of him, using my body weight to drive him to the ground. His head smacked into the asphalt with a wet thud, and as his eyes went glassy, I smashed my gun into the bridge of his nose, putting him out.

Mary Ann's scream still rang in my ears, but I pushed down the need to run back to her for a moment. The last time had nearly gotten me killed. Part of me expected to hear sirens, but I didn't. That wasn't good. It meant that for one reason or another the police were ignoring a firefight in the middle of the suburbs.

Damn.

Confident the thug beneath me was down for the count, I relieved him of his AK47 and got to my feet. This time, I glanced inside the SUV but didn't see anyone but the dead driver.

As I turned back toward the house, I went to holster my empty Glock and realized I was still in my puppy dog boxers. A grunt of annoyance escaped me as I dropped the Glock to the ground, hoping I could recover it later and made my way forward with the AK47.

As soon as I got close to the garage, two more thugs shot at me from the back door of the structure, but the AK was more than enough to turn them to mincemeat.

I relieved them of their weapons and slung one over my shoulder. I made my way forward, one AK47 in each hand. Part of me didn't really like the Russian weapons, but they were good for getting beat to hell and still firing, so I hoped they would work even if accuracy was more spray and pray.

As I ventured back into the house, I kept careful aim. The last thing I wanted to do was shoot at a thug and kill Mary Ann... if that happened.

No. That couldn't be allowed.

I had to find her.

Another scream tore through the house, coming from the back room. I glanced down the hall, and seeing no one, I made my way forward. A quick glance in the bathroom made my mouth fall open. The tiny room was thrashed. The pictures knocked off the walls. Broken glass from their frames and the shattered mirror was spilled across the tile. I swallowed hard. What had happened here?

I didn't have time for that. I pushed down my emotions and made my way out of the hall.

There were only two more rooms in this hallway, my dad's trophy room and his bedroom.

A quick glance in the trophy room revealed all the awards I'd ever won along with my dad's fishing and sailing knickknacks. No one inside, and it struck me cold. What if they were in the bedroom because, well…

I grunted, forcing down a sudden bout of rage, and spun on my heel, racing toward the master bedroom. I couldn't hear much inside, but that didn't matter because I could see a bloody handprint on the door. That wasn't good.

I pushed it open slowly and found myself looking at the back of a tattooed thug with a bald head. He had a roll of duct tape in one hand and was busy trying to force Mary Ann's arms together. She was kicking and clawing and trying her best to fight him off, but it didn't seem to have a lot of effect from my vantage point.

No matter.

As the guy grabbed hold of her wrists and wrenched her forward, I pressed the barrel of the AK47 to the back of his skull.

"No means no, dirtbag," I said and pulled the trigger. His life evaporated in a spray of blood and bone, and as his body started to slump, I pushed him off the bed and onto the floor. Crimson oozed out of his ruined head, spreading into a puddle around him, but I ignored it as I pulled Mary Ann into my arms.

"I'm so sorry," I said as she cried into my chest. "I never should have left you here."

"You saved me... he... he was..." she mumbled through sobs.

"I know. It's okay." A cruel smile broke out across my face. "He won't hurt anyone, anymore."

"That's unfortunate, Mr. Ryder," said a voice right before a gun barrel pressed right between my shoulder blades. "See, I knew Max was dumb enough to play the bait," the voice continued, "but I'm still sad to see him go."

I whirled as he fired, feeling the sting of the bullet as it tore superficially into my back. The guy leapt backward, trying to bring his gun back around, but I countered by kicking his wrist.

He grunted, dropping his Beretta, and took a step back to bring his hands up. He was a bigger dude with skin the color of three-day-old coffee and a sneer just as angry. He wore a really nice suit with a white shirt underneath and a blue bowtie.

"I'd hoped for the easy way, but I guess that's not happening." He raised his ham-sized fists and threw a jab through the air so fast the wind of it buffeted against my face. The guy was quick. That was fine, I'd dealt with lots of quick guys before. The key was to hit them really hard.

He lunged at me, and I took a step back, trying to dodge. My legs hit the bed, and I stumbled. His knuckles collided with my nose. Blood and pain exploded from my face, and my eyes went blurry as he reared back to punch me again.

The blow came, knocking me to the ground. I tried to crawl away, and as I did, he kicked me hard in the stomach. My breath burst from my mouth in a spray of spittle. As I flopped onto my side, I saw him reach into his pocket and pull out a six-inch Buck knife.

"When you see your dad in hell, give him my regards," he said, flipping open his knife and smiling at me.

I kicked at him, my heel catching him in the shin. He stumbled, but there wasn't enough force behind the blow to make him do more. I tried to get to my feet, and as I did, he slashed at me. I dodged, narrowly, but hit the dresser with my hip. Pain nearly made my knees buckle as I reached out, grabbing onto it to steady myself.

"Nowhere to go," he said, raising his knife to deliver the final blow, and as I debated trying to block it anyway, his head exploded into a spray of blood that covered my face and neck in hot sticky fluid.

As his body crumpled to the ground, I saw Mary Ann standing behind him. The assassin's

Beretta was clenched in her shaking hands. Her whole body started to tremble as she slumped to her knees, dropping the gun.

CHAPTER 15

"It'll be okay," I said while I maneuvered the Tahoe down the street. My dad's bullet-riddled house was fading in the rearview. As I watched it go, a sense of dread welled up from my stomach. My dad might actually be dead. No, I couldn't believe that was true. Not for a second.

Still as much as I tried to push it out of my mind and refocus on finding him, worry plagued my thoughts. Guys who shot up a house in the middle of the day wouldn't give a damn about killing my father, and worse? The police hadn't come. Hell, I still didn't hear sirens. That meant the police probably worked for them. Sure, there were probably a few good ones. For all I knew, that was most of them, but someone had kept them from showing up.

"It's not okay," Mary Ann whispered from next to me. Her voice was so soft, it made me think of a broken angel. "I killed a man, Billy. I pulled the trigger and shot him. God, I feel sick." My heart went out to her as she turned her tear-strewn face away from me and stared out the passenger window like she could find answers there.

"That's how you know you're a good person. Trust me, killing is never easy. It tears you up inside, but the thing is, you sort of want it to do that because if you can take someone's life without it meaning anything, without it cutting you up like a big bag of glass, that's when you know you're gone for good," I said, reaching out to touch her leg with one hand.

The moment I did, she jumped like an electric shock had run through her body. She turned, looking at my hand. Then, instead of pulling away, she put her hand over mine. Hers was warm and comforting and was shaking like a leaf.

"I suppose you're right." She shook her head and wiped her eyes with her free hand. "My God, Billy Ryder. You come back into my life for less than a day, and already I'm killing people." She shook her head once more like she was trying to dismiss the thought. When she finished, her eyes settled on me with all the seriousness of a mama bear protecting her cubs. "What are we going to do now?"

"I'm not sure, really," I said, shaking my head as I turned onto the main street and headed in a direction that could only be classified as away. "I'd planned on camping out at Pop's house until my buddy showed up." I nodded toward the laptop and phone sitting in the back. "But right now, much as I hate to admit it, I don't have anywhere to go." I slapped the steering wheel with my palm. "Destination unknown, I guess."

"Well, you can't play in the mud and expect not to get dirty, I suppose," she said, biting her lip as she stared up at the ceiling in thought. "You really think your friend can help find your dad?"

"That I don't know." I took a deep breath and let it out slowly. "There might not be anything on that laptop."

"You have to have faith, Billy," she said, and as the silence settled around us like a thick blanket, she continued. "'Sides, if I know Bob Ryder, I'd be willing to bet he's waiting for you somewhere. Hell, he's probably got 'em right where he wants 'em." She gave me a tough smile as she ran a hand through her hair, brushing it behind her ear. "But you didn't really answer my question."

"How's that?" I asked, glancing over my shoulder to look for tails. So far, I hadn't seen anyone, but that didn't mean there weren't any. Part of me wanted to ditch the Tahoe. It was likely the Scorpions knew what it looked like, but that'd leave me with even fewer options. Right now, I needed to stay mobile.

"I asked if your friend can really help you," she said, looking over at me. "The one you were waiting for. What's he do exactly?"

I sighed. "He's a guy I met way back in the Corps. Real nice guy, and a whiz with computers. Went to college after he got out and was hired on for some weird security company." I took a deep breath. "The long and short of it is, if there's anything on that computer, he'll get it out."

"And what's the plan then?" she asked, raising an eyebrow. "You go take on all the Scorpions?"

"Pretty much," I said, gritting my teeth as I turned left, causing pain to stab through my ribs. The adrenaline had mostly faded, and now my good friends, pain and stiffness, had taken their places.

"That's a silly plan," she said, squeezing my fingers. "But it does sound like a Billy Ryder plan." She looked at me pointedly. "You can't do that alone."

"It's my dad. I can't ask anyone to come help." I gritted my teeth. He was my responsibility, and I couldn't ask others to take on that burden, that risk, for me. "You know why I hate a lot of movies?"

"Because they're terribly made or rehashed remakes?" she asked, peering quizzically at me.

"Well, there is that." I shook my head. "It's 'cause you always see the movies where the guy gets his friends, and they go take on the bad guys to save one guy. Like, you know, Private Ryan. Then everyone gets killed trying to save the one guy. It's just a horrible trade when you consider all lives are special." I sighed. "I won't let my friends trade their lives for my dad."

"But those people chose to do that, to make that trade," she said, biting her lip again. "I think your friends probably would too."

"That's the problem. I could call Max and Vicky. They would come charge inside with me, and maybe get themselves killed. They'd do it of their own free will, sure thing, but I can't let them. I won't trade them for my dad." I turned right, angling onto a street that had a Superstore on its right about two blocks up. "Not when I can get him out on my own. Assuming he's still alive."

"You have to assume he's still alive or this is a waste," she said, lifting her hand to touch my face. "But I understand where you're coming from. It's damned crazy, but I get it."

"Good, I'm glad," I said, turning to look at her and finding her staring right at me, her eyes piercing all the way to my soul, and the weird thing was, they seemed okay with what it found there.

"So, let's go to my place." She nodded emphatically. "Face it, you can't just drive around all day, and you can't go to your dad's." She gestured toward the car as if to make a point. "And they don't know who I am. It's the safest place to go and wait."

"Unless your boyfriend is a Scorpion —"

My statement was cut off by a derisive snort from Mary Ann. "Chuck might be a lot of things, but he's hardly a Scorpion."

"Still, I don't like the idea of putting you in danger," I said as I pulled into the parking lot of the Supercenter and parked in the middle. It was mostly empty, which concerned me because it made my Tahoe easier to find.

"I'm already in danger, or did you miss the part where I shot a guy," she said as I unfastened my seatbelt. That was an excellent point, and one I couldn't argue with. "Do you need something here?" she added, glancing around and scrunching up her nose.

"Just a parking space," I said, getting out of the car and coming around to her side. I had the door open as she was unfastening her seat belt. "I'm worried they can follow the Tahoe."

"Does that mean we're walking?" she asked, casting quick, furtive glances around the parking lot as she got out.

"That depends," I said, taking her hand and

leading her toward the bus stop. "How far do you live from here?"

"Far enough that I'll call an Uber," she said, pulling out her phone. She stared at it a minute before pulling her other hand out of mine.

"Okay," I said, nodding to her as I glanced around. "Do it from the donut shop across the street." I pointed. "Just to be safe."

CHAPTER 16

About twenty minutes later, we pulled up in front of one of those crummy apartment buildings in the even crummier side of town. Graffiti littered the dilapidated walls, and litter overflowed out of the dumpster just hidden in the alley to the left of the building. The building looked like it might have been nice a decade before, but years of neglect and disuse had made it well, less so.

As I exited the car and moved to open Mary Ann's door, I noticed a shiny black BMW Roadster sitting out front. It seemed a little odd, and I must have stopped to look at it for longer than I'd thought because the next thing I knew Mary Ann was outside the car and standing next to me.

"What is it?" she asked, her gaze following

mine to rest on the car, and as her eyes settled on it, she went absolutely ballistic. "Why that no good..." She stomped forward, hands clenched into fists.

As she moved forward, the BMW's driver's side door opened to reveal the cowboy from earlier. He wasn't wearing his stupid hat, but the rest of him was mostly the same. He began moving forward, an armful of roses held out in front of himself like a shield.

"Go away!" Mary Ann snapped, glaring at him as she came up short. "I don't want your flowers."

"Look, babe, you know I get mad sometimes..." he said, holding the flowers out toward her. "But, you know I care for you."

"No, you don't. You just like having someone you can kick around," she said, crossing her arms over her chest and glaring at him hard enough to make me want to flinch even though her anger wasn't even directed at me.

Behind me, the driver of the black CRV took off, no doubt headed to his next pick up. I watched him go for a second before turning back to watch the scene unfold. A sense of protectiveness flashed through me at the sight of Chuck. Part of me wanted to step in and beat the guy into the pavement on principle, but from the way Mary Ann was looking at him, I was pretty sure she didn't need nor want my help.

"That's not true, babe." He moved closer, and as he reached out to her with his free hand, Mary Ann pushed his hand away.

"Don't touch me." She shook her head. "Go away, Chuck."

"I won't," he replied, malice settling across his features as his gaze flitted to me. "What, you think 'cause this guy saved you in a bar, he's going to put up with you? Newsflash, he won't. He'll be gone the second he realizes what a screw-up you are!" Part of me couldn't believe he'd actually said that to her, but most of me knew why he had. He was a scum bag who made himself feel better by beating up women.

"Maybe," Mary Ann said, her voice edged with hurt. "But I don't need him or you." She took a step toward him and shoved him, causing the roses to fall to the ground. They hit with a thwap before spraying outward in an explosion of petals and leaves. "I don't need any man to make me feel special, and I can handle my own crap." Her eyes sparkled with rage. "I know that now."

"Well, it's nice to see you've got a backbone. Too bad it's holding up a bunch of crap." Chuck's hands tensed, and for a second, I thought I'd have to step in. Then he glanced over at me and shook his head sadly. "Partner, I hope you know what you've gotten yourself into." Then he turned on his heel and strode back toward his car. Without another word, he got inside and took off with a squeal of rubber that was rivaled only by the explosion of bass coming from within the vehicle.

"You okay?" I asked, coming toward her as she watched him go. She nodded, not looking at me. Then she shook her entire body. It was a little weird because when she was done, she strode forward, chin held high even though I could see tears threatening to spill from her eyes.

"Yeah, come on." She looked back at me, and her face was a stony mask. "Let's get inside before people see you. While the place might not be much, I would like my security deposit back some day."

"I can hear that," I said, following her toward the building. She pressed a code into the keypad beside the door. The light next to the door turned from red to green, and the sound of a magnetic lock opening filled my ears. She pulled the door open, holding it long enough for me to grab it before stepping inside.

"Damn." She tossed a frown at the elevator. "Guess we're walking."

"Has the elevator been broken for a while?" I asked, noting the faded, tattered edges of the "out of order" sign duct-taped to the doors. "'Cause that sign seems pretty old."

"Pretty much the whole time I've lived here, and yet I still hope..." she trailed off as she headed toward the stairs. "I'm only on the third floor though, so it isn't so bad."

I nodded, following her into the stairwell. As we reached her floor, I knew two things. My body had been too beat to hell to tolerate stairs, and I'd gotten a bit too soft since my time in the Corps.

As she unlocked the door to Apartment 3B, she shot me a nervous smile. "It's a mess, sorry."

"I'm sure it's just perfect," I said as she pushed open the door. "Anywhere with you is."

"Billy Ryder, you keep saying things like that to me, and I might just think you're flirting," she said, before laughing. "And I know Billy Ryder doesn't flirt."

"True," I said as she stepped inside and gestured for me to follow. The room beyond the threshold was clean in that lived in way, which was to say there weren't dishes on the small table by the couch table, and the floor was relatively clutter free. Just beyond, I could see the kitchen counter was piled with dirty dishes and stacks of old mail that had slowly accumulated.

"It's not much, but it's home," she said, gesturing nervously around the room.

"I love the green couches," I said, moving

forward and touching one with my index finger. It was surprisingly soft and looked to be made of real leather despite being lime green.

"I got those at a garage sale for fifty bucks." She bit her lip. "Most of my stuff is from a thrift store or garage sales, actually." She pointed to the table. "That's from Craigslist." She smirked. "I call it Craig."

"Well, Craig has lots of character," I said, glancing at the scarred cherry-wood table. Like the building, it'd probably been nice when it was new, but not so much now.

"That's an interesting way of putting that," she said, moving into the kitchen. "I know you're in a hurry, but it seems to me, we've got a couple hours to kill right? You want something to eat?"

"Sure," I said, nodding at her as I sat down on the couch. "I'm sure my friend will call soon enough."

"Okay, I'll make some sandwiches," she said, opening the fridge and looking around. It sort of made me glad because I was beginning to worry that if we stopped to talk about everything that'd happened, it'd just wind up stretching into an awkward silence I wouldn't be able to deal with. Sandwiches though? That, I could handle.

"Do you need help?" I asked, and as I started to get up, she chided me.

"I'm a big girl. I can make two PB & Js

without your help. Just sit there, and try not to bleed on my stuff." A moment later, she set a cold Corona and a paper plate with a sandwich on it down in front of me. "Eat up. I'm going to go shower and change." She nodded to me once, and I saw the edge of her mask slip just a bit, and I instantly knew she just wanted alone time. That was fine though.

"Sure thing," I replied, picking up the beer and taking a sip. "I'll just be out here trying not to bleed."

"Good," she said, and with that, she disappeared into the bedroom.

CHAPTER 17

"Billy, wake up," Mary Ann whispered, shaking me out of a dream I couldn't quite remember. As my eyes fluttered open to see her smiling face hovering over me, I yawned. Loudly.

"Sorry," I mumbled, sitting back and wiping my eyes with the back of one hand. "Must have fallen asleep."

"I noticed," she said, grinning at me as she sat down on the couch beside me. "Your friend called a few minutes ago. I answered, hope that's okay." She shot me a sheepish smile, and I shrugged. It didn't really bother me that she'd answered my phone, but I was annoyed I'd missed it because I'd been asleep. I had a mission and wasting time asleep wouldn't help me find my dad.

"It's fine," I grumbled, stifling another yawn. "What'd he say?"

"He'll meet us at the Corner Bistro in fifteen minutes." She handed me my phone. "It's about ten minutes from here on Olive."

I rubbed my eyes again, trying to get the fog out of my brain. It didn't work.

"Okay. We'd better get a move on then," I said, getting to my feet while trying to ignore how my body ached like I'd just gone ten rounds with Mohammed Ali.

"There's coffee in the kitchen. Want some?" Mary Ann asked, getting to her feet and smoothing her black skirt over her knees. She was wearing black yoga pants beneath it and a baby blue t-shirt that made me think she'd been poured into it.

"If it's quick," I said, glancing at my watch. "I don't want to be late." It was almost four. I'd been out a while. A sharp pang of worry shot through me. Hopefully, I hadn't missed my chance to save dad because I'd been napping.

"It's already done," she said as I tore my gaze from the watch. "Here." Mary Ann shoved a travel mug full of black coffee into my hands. I took a deep breath, inhaling the scent and smiled. "Best part of waking up, eh Billy?" She winked at me before she headed toward the door. "Come on, let's get out of here."

"You're not coming," I said so suddenly I

nearly spat out the coffee in my mouth. I took a deep breath and wiped my mouth with the back of my hand as she gave me a strange, confused look. "I mean, you can't—"

"Billy Ryder, are you trying to tell," she touched her chest with one slender finger, "a grown ass woman, what she can and cannot do?" She cocked an angry eyebrow at me.

"No, ma'am," I said and sipped my coffee instead of arguing with her. I'd learned long ago that no good ever came from arguing with women, and Mary Ann had never struck me as an exception in that regard. Besides, I didn't have time for it. If she wanted to come, she could come.

"Good because I'd hate to think you'd gone dense during the last few years." She smiled at me, and for a second, I thought someone had turned on the sun. "Well, denser. You did leave me, after all." It was weird because her eyes sparkled with sadness as she said the last part.

And, even though I knew I needed to focus on finding my dad, my throat choked up a bit as I remembered all the things we'd done together. As I stood there in her crummy apartment looking at her, I couldn't help but think that in my haste to escape this town, I'd left a good chunk of myself behind. Worse, I hadn't even known it was missing until now.

"I'm sorry," I said before I could stop

myself. "I shouldn't have left."

"I agree," she said, opening the door. "And while I'm not quite tired of hearing you apologize for it, we need to get a move on." She stepped through the threshold. "Come on."

"Yes, ma'am," I replied, taking a swig of coffee as I followed her out.

A few moments later, we were sitting inside her old Toyota Camry. In addition to being clean and smelling like blueberries and cream, it would get us where we needed to go quick enough. That was what mattered.

"You're awfully quiet," she said as we pulled onto the street and made out way toward the Corner Bistro where my buddy Ren waited for us.

"Just thinking," I said, patting the laptop in my lap. It had to get me to my dad, had to unlock the key of where the Scorpions had him. "This might all be for nothing. If the info isn't on this thing..."

"It will be," she said, and her enthusiasm was practically contagious.

For a minute, I almost believed her. Unfortunately, even if she was right, I didn't know exactly what the Scorpions were up to, but chances were good they'd kill to protect it.

"I hope you're right," I replied as she switched on the radio, filling the tiny car with Jimmy Buffett. "'Cause if not, I'm going to have to try to find Mr. Elliott and make him talk. Something tells me that isn't going to go well for any of us."

"Hopefully, it won't come to that," she said as the silence stretched around us. "I'm sure that computer will hold the key to finding your dad, Billy."

I didn't reply. I didn't need to keep up this conversation. Instead, I stared out the window and tried not to think my dad was already dead. I didn't know what he'd been up to, but assuming he hadn't been killed in the opening salvo, I was willing to bet he had something they wanted. After all, why else would his boat have been ransacked?

I just hoped it was enough to keep him alive until I found him.

That thought stuck in my brain until we pulled into the strip mall that housed the Corner Bistro. The building was bright yellow with eves done in neon pink, and there was a line halfway down the block.

"Is it always this crowded?" I asked, glancing at Mary Ann as she parked way in the back between a huge black Dodge Charger and a white Subaru Forrester.

"Yes, but I called ahead, so hopefully our name got put down." She waved off her statement. "It'll be fine. I know a guy." She smiled at me and touched my arm. "Wow, I've always wanted to say that."

I laughed. Couldn't help it.

As we made our way through the parking lot and pushed through the door, I saw Ren tucked back in a corner booth by himself. He was one of those thin guys that always reminded me of a spider. His oversized T-shirt hung on his scarecrow frame like a bad joke.

As we approached, he looked up from his mountain of pancakes and smiled at me before running a hand through his slicked-back black hair. Then he seemed to remember himself and hopped to his feet.

"A pleasure," he said, reaching out and taking Mary Ann's hand. He brushed his lips across it before releasing her and shoving his hand toward me. "You, less so."

"Thanks for coming, Ren," I said, taking his hand and shaking it. He squeezed, but not hard. No, it was a firm, confident shake that let me know he had nothing to prove.

"I wouldn't miss it for the world, Billy." He nodded to the laptop as he slid back into the booth. "That the laptop?"

"Yeah," I said, handing it over to him before following Mary into the booth. "Can you make it sing?"

"Like a goddamned canary," Ren said, taking the laptop from me. He flipped it open, grabbed the screwdriver off his ear, and unscrewed the case. A second later, the laptop's guts were strewn across the table, and he had part of it hooked up to another computer he'd pulled from his backpack.

"You two need a minute, or are you ready to order?" the red-headed twenty-something waitress asked before popping her gum. As I turned toward her, I realized I'd not bothered to look at a menu. My mouth fell open as I tried to think of what to do when Mary Ann saved the day.

"Two iced teas, and two specials," she said, and the waitress nodded.

"You want house sauce?" the waitress asked, scribbling it on her pad.

"Of course," Mary Ann said, nodding. "Why else would we come here?"

"Fair enough," the waitress replied, shrugging. "Be back in a bit with your drinks." She shot us a smile that fractured at the edges as she looked over Ren, who was too busy fiddling with the disemboweled laptop to notice.

"Thanks," I said, and as she walked away, I turned to Mary Ann. "What's the special?"

"Chicken fried steak, hash browns, bacon, and three fried eggs." As she spoke, my mouth actually watered. It was crazy because I was starving, but then again, my body was beaten to hell. I definitely needed some calories, even if my gut wanted to argue the point a bit.

"That sounds kind of amazing," I replied as Ren looked up with a huge grin on his face.

"Boomshakalaka!" he said, smacking the table with one hand. "I'm in. Their security is amateur hour."

"That was fast," I said, scratching my cheek. "So I'm trying to find my dad, anything about that in there?"

Ren got quiet for a minute before slowly shaking his head. "Nothing like that. This all seems fairly mundane. There's talk of a ship coming in, but nothing else... interesting." He shrugged. "Lots of email and stuff. Could take a while to go through."

"Why's the ship seem interesting?" I asked as the waitress set down our drinks before hurrying off.

"The Hard Tide? Only cause there's a few emails about it." He stopped and moved back to his main machine and typed something in. "Oh. That's why."

"What?" I said before taking a sip of the iced tea. I hadn't realized how thirsty I was, and now that I had taken a sip, I realized I could down the whole thing without trying.

"It's probably loaded with drugs." Ren looked at me as if begging me to ask him to elaborate.

"Why is that?" I asked even though part of me didn't care. I already knew they were bad guys, but at the same time, knowing more about my enemy, might make it easier to beat them and find my dad.

"It's just a pattern. A lot of these numbers look bogus. You can tell from the pattern of the way the transactions work. Humans always seem like they're doing stuff randomly, but most often, they don't actually do things randomly." He waved off the comment. "I could explain it, but ultimately, it doesn't matter. My point is that I'm almost one hundred percent certain these guys are mega drug dealers, and that means they'll have tough security."

"How's that help us? Do you know what security they'll have?" I asked, rolling it over in my brain. Sure, they might be tough, but at the end of the day, they were working for money.

"Security? Not really, but that boat, the Hard Tide? It comes in tonight. Like midnight tonight, and will be gone in the morning." He spun his laptop around to show me the docking records he'd pulled up.

"Who owns it?" I asked, rubbing my chin. The Hard Tide wasn't my dad, but I was willing to bet it'd definitely have something on it the Scorpions would be willing to trade for him.

"A shell corporation called Cooper Investments." Ren shrugged and began tapping at his computer. "Okay, that's a shell corporation owned by another company." He bit his lip and began tapping away, his eyes focused with concentration. "All right, I've got an address for a dude named Elliott Cline. Not sure who he is, but I'd go talk to him. I'll text you the address." Ren pulled out his phone. "I'm willing to bet he knows exactly who has your dad. I'll keep working on this and see if I can find anything. After that, I'm gonna send this to my buddy in the FBI narcotics division. It'll be like Christmas for him."

"Okay. Well, that gives us a starting point." I stopped, about to ask him why he'd suggested Elliott Cline when the name struck me like a brick. Was that the guy Jack had spoken with on the phone? I was willing to bet it was, and even better, he'd probably know where my dad was since Tom worked for him. If not, I was going to bet he knew who would.

CHAPTER 18

"If someone comes out here, just shoot them," I said, trying to smile as I spoke so as to not frighten Mary Ann. Part of me wanted her to be scared though. It'd make her more cautious. We were half a block away from the Blazing Realty building, which had rented office space to one, Elliott Cline. While I wasn't absolutely sure it was him, Ren rarely steered me wrong, and never on purpose.

"I'm not sure I could do that again..." she mumbled, looking at the Beretta we'd taken from the gunman. Part of me had wanted to dump it, but I figured the guy would have gone to enough trouble to keep it off the grid, and she needed a weapon.

"I hate to say this, but it gets easier." I nodded to the gun. "Just don't get hurt. I'll be back as soon as I can," I said, and she nodded.

"Be careful, Billy." She swallowed hard and picked up the gun, cradling it in her hands before hiding it in her purse.

"I will," I said before adjusting my UPD cap and putting the big cardboard box under my arm. Then I walked down the block toward Blazing Realty doing my best delivery boy impression.

A moment later, I was stepping into the air-conditioned building and walking toward the pretty little thing busily avoiding everyone inside as she looked at the mess of papers strewn across her desk.

"Hello," I said, flashing my best million dollar smile at her as I dropped the box onto her desk. "I've got a package for Elliott Cline in suite twelve." I glanced at my clipboard. "It's on floor three, I believe."

"You're not the usual guy," she said, looking up at me before glancing at the box. "Where's James?"

"We swapped shifts. He needed to go to the doctors or help a doctor, or something." I shrugged as I offered her the clipboard. "I'm really late, you think you could help me out and take this up?"

She raised an eyebrow at me as she signed for the package. "I suppose I could…" She trailed off as she saw the "please deliver to occupant" notice. "Actually, you'll have to deliver this one yourself." She tapped the notice, her cheeks flushing. "Sorry."

"It's okay," I said, sighing like I was lifting the weight of the world as I grabbed the box, and made to go toward the elevator. "Guess it's only a few more minutes till quitting time. Man, I can practically taste those half-priced wings."

She shook her head at me as I thumbed the up button for the elevator and waited. A moment later, it dinged, and I stepped inside. As the elevator lifted, I let out a sigh. I hadn't known what to expect by way of resistance. So far, so good, but that could change any moment.

The elevator dinged a moment later, and the doors opened to reveal the hallway toward floor three. Like on the first floor, there was a lady sitting at a receptionist's desk. A sign behind her read Cline Import and Export in flowing green script. The rest of the floor was closed off behind a wall with a large unmarked door.

"Can I help you?" the brunette receptionist asked as I strode forward and put the box down on her desk.

"Just got a delivery for Mr. Cline in suite twelve." I nodded toward the door. "Do you want me to take it to him?" I asked, offering her the clipboard.

"No," she said flatly before taking the

clipboard and scribbling her name on the line. "I'll take it."

"Um... I would love to let you, but I really need to take it there." I pointed at the notice.

"That won't be possible," she said, reaching for the package.

"Oh, it's no problem," I said, swiping it off the desk and moving past her toward the door. Before she could stop me, I twisted the knob, thanked God it opened, and shouldered my way inside.

"Sir!" she cried, but I was already through. I made my way forward, ignoring all the people in the room. Most of them looked like regular guys in suits, but there were a couple bigger folks. The kinds of guys who looked like they chewed iron and spat nails.

"Sir!" the receptionist repeated as I strode forward in my UPD greens like I ran the place.

"Yes?" I replied, glancing over my shoulder as I reached into my pocket.

"Nancy, is this guy doing something wrong?" a big palooka to my left said as I moved toward suite twelve. It was just a few meters away and was clearly bigger than the rest of the offices. The name Cline was stenciled across the burnished glass door. While the rest of the office was made of similarly opaque glass, I could tell there was someone inside standing over the desk.

"I'm just delivering a package," I said as

Nancy practically broke out into a run, her high heels clomping on the tile floor.

"Just wait a second," Nancy practically shrieked, and this time more people turned to see what was going on as the big guy started coming toward me, hands curled into fists.

"Okay, okay," I said, stopping and holding out the box. "What's the big deal?" Nancy stared at me for a second, her mouth half open as I took another slow step toward the office and lifted the box. "You need to call ahead and let him know he needs to sign for this or something?"

"Yes, exactly," Nancy said, regaining control of the situation, and as she spoke, the room settled. "But since you're here already, I guess I'll just do it manually." She huffed out an annoyed breath and marched past me toward the office. Then she knocked lightly on the door.

"Yes?" asked the voice from within. The same one I'd spoken with on the phone. "What is it?"

Nancy pushed the door open a crack and stuck her mousy head inside. "Sorry, sir, but there's a UPD guy here. He's insisting you need to sign for this package personally."

Cline was silent for a moment before running a hand through his hair. "You know this is exactly what I pay you to deal with, right?" he said before sighing. "Fine, whatever.

Send him in."

Nancy glared at me as she nodded. "Come in, Mr....?"

"Conner," I said, shrugging.

"Well, hurry up, Mr. Conner," the guy inside said. "I haven't got all day."

"Sorry, sir," I said and made my way forward. I was so close to Elliott, I could practically taste it. Nancy stepped out of the way and allowed me inside before disappearing as the door swung shut behind me.

I reached up and adjusted my green UPD cap before moving toward Elliott. I didn't know why I was worried. The white-haired guy barely looked up at me before going back to his computer.

"So what's so important?" the guy asked as I handed him the clipboard.

"You know how protocol is," I said with a shrug as he took the clipboard.

"Say, aren't these usually electronic?" he asked, glancing up at me as I reached into the holster hidden behind my back and pulled my Glock free. His eyes went wide as I pointed it at his face. Then they narrowed. "You're making a big mistake."

"You're going to tell me where my dad is," I said, moving around the desk so I had his entire body within view.

"You must be Mr. Ryder. I should have

known." He nodded once and put his hands flat on his thighs. He was wearing a black suit that probably cost more than I made in a month.

"So where is he?" I asked, taking care to keep enough distance between us so he couldn't easily knock my gun away.

"Probably spilling his guts to Jimmy." Elliott shrugged. "He took something that isn't his, and the owner wants it back."

The urge to wring his neck until his eyes popped out of his skull filled me, but that wouldn't help me. No, I had to stick to the plan and get information.

"And where do I find Jimmy?" I growled, making sure to keep the gun sighted on his smug face.

"You don't find Jimmy. He finds you." The guy smiled, and without thinking, I smacked him with the gun. His head snapped sideways, but he stifled a cry. When he looked back at me, his lip was busted open. He touched it casually with his index finger.

"I'm not going to ask again, Elliott."

"That's going to cost you, Mr. Ryder," Elliott said, staring at his finger. His lips twitched into the barest smile. "Fine, it's your funeral." He reached out and pulled a pen from the cup on his desk and wrote down an address on a slip of paper. He slid it across the desk.

"Thanks," I said, nodding to him as I picked it up. A quick glance told me it was across town, but not much else.

"You're welcome," he said and then moved to turn back to his desk as I pocketed the address. "Now, if you don't mind, I have some work to do."

"Gonna let me out of here just like that?" I asked, raising an eyebrow.

"Do you know how hard it is to get blood out of the grout in the floor?" He waved off the statement. "Of course you don't. So yes, walk out, Mr. Ryder. I'll catch up with you later." His eyes glinted with hidden steel. "Count on that."

His words probably should have worried me, but at the moment, I had a lead. I couldn't focus on this guy. In the grand scheme of things, what he wanted probably wouldn't matter much anyway.

"Fair enough," I said, turning and walking away. I hadn't gotten what I'd wanted, but I had another lead.

I hit the office door, but Elliott was already ignoring me as he focused on his computer, but that was fine, I had a person to find and an address.

As I made my way back toward the elevator, Nancy glanced at me. "I'm glad you weren't up to anything untoward," she said, giving me an apologetic smile.

I nodded to her as the package I'd left in Elliott's office exploded, blowing his office out across the street below.

CHAPTER 19

As I made my way down the stairs, chaos, confusion, and fire consumed the building. I tried to ignore my heart pounding in my chest. The homemade charge I'd planted in Elliott's office had worked like a charm, flinging the son of a gun's body out into the fresh air several stories up, but causing little other collateral damage.

That didn't mean I wanted to stick around and let people put together the pieces. As fire alarms blared in my ears, I hustled out of the stairwell, shouldering open the door and stepping into the throng of other people desperately trying to flee the building. While I was fairly sure the fire sprinklers had already put out the blaze, part of me worried about the people who worked here anyway.

I wasn't sure how many people here actually worked for the Scorpions, but I couldn't think about that now. The look in Elliott's eyes as he told me we'd meet up later was burned into my brain. Those were the eyes of a predator, and what's more, he'd caught my scent. We'd both known it.

Killing him had been the right call because if I'd learned one thing dealing with insurgents, it was that the easiest way to win was to cut the head off the snake. Then the rest of it would flail uselessly. So far, I'd cut off two heads, and while I wasn't sure how many were left, I knew it couldn't be many.

Besides, I had another name and an address. The illustrious Jimmy. I'd find him and break him. Only, I'd have to be more careful because they might be expecting me.

As I broke through the lobby doors with the crowd, I spun on my heel and headed toward my meeting place with Mary Ann. The sounds of police sirens filled my ears, and as I glanced toward the sound, I saw the cars streaking toward the building, gumballs flashing.

Adrenaline surged through my veins, and I had to fight the urge to run. If I did that, someone might chase me, and that was the last thing I needed. Instead, I tucked my hands into the pockets of my green UPD shorts and tried to look as nonchalant as possible.

As I came to the corner, I turned and

glanced around to see if anyone had followed me. No one had.

I sucked in a breath and tried to calm myself as I pulled off my cap and ran a hand through my sweaty hair. Part of me was surprised the bomb had worked, what with it having been jury-rigged and all, but it looked like when it came to bombs, Ren knew a thing or two.

I moved down the street, my sneakers pounding on the sidewalk as I rolled over my plan in my head. First thing was first, I needed to find out about this Jimmy.

I pulled out my cellphone and hit Ren's number. It rang twice before he picked up.

"I don't have anything yet," Ren said by way of hello.

"I have a first name and an address for you," I said, giving him the information on Jimmy I'd gotten from Elliott. "Anything about him in there."

"Let me check," Ren said, and he got quiet for a second. "Yeah, oh… that guy's bad. He's a fixer. You know the type, right?"

"That's who they said had my dad." I took a deep breath, trying to staunch the worry in my gut.

"Maybe they're lying?" Ren replied, strain in his voice. "Look, the address they gave me is legit. I'd start there, but the dude's a ghost. Not a Scorpion, but a hired merc. He'll fade to nothing if you don't get him now."

"Gotcha," I said as Mary Ann pulled up next to me. I nodded at her as I hung up the phone and got in.

"Get anything?" she asked as I stripped off the UPD shirt and tossed it in the backseat, leaving me sitting there in my undershirt. I reached under the seat and pulled out a dusk gray T-shirt and pulled it on.

"I got this. Leads to a fixer named Jimmy." I slid the sheet of paper Elliott had given me with Jimmy's address on it to Mary Ann. She looked at it for a second and nodded.

"That's not exactly a safe part of town," she said as she guided the car into traffic and away from the cluster I'd created a few blocks away.

"Don't have much of a choice. Word is he knows about my dad. 'Sides, I haven't got any other leads."

"I see what you're doing," Mary Ann said, her grip tightening around the steering wheel until her knuckles went white. "Now, rest a moment. We'll be there soon."

"I'll do my best," I whispered before my eyes shut of their own accord.

What felt like seconds later, we pulled up in front of a Terrific Tom's Pizza and Waffles. I glanced at her, confused as I tried to blink away my impromptu nap.

"We're here," she said, parking the car.

"I can see that." I gestured at the building. "But why are we here?"

"This is where you told me to come." She pointed at the note, and I realized she was right. The address I'd been given belonged to the pizza place. That seemed crazy, and I'd have thought Elliott had played me, but Ren had corroborated the address.

"Great," I mumbled as I checked my surroundings. There weren't many other cars in the lot even for the other businesses, a pawn shop and a laundromat. "This is going to be fun."

"Be careful," Mary Ann said, and as she leaned toward the passenger seat to wave me good luck, a pang of fear washed down my throat. I couldn't let her stay here in the open, nor get out where they might see us together.

"Drive away," I said, meeting her eyes. "I'll call when I need you." As her face screwed up in annoyance, I continued. "Seriously. You're like the only car here, and for all I know, cameras are watching us right now. Get out of here, fast."

"Okay," she said, putting the car back into gear and taking off, racing out of the parking lot and merging into the nearly non-existent traffic. I could see concern etched across her face as she wove into the left lane and threw on her blinker.

We drove about half a block farther in silence. Thankfully, I spotted a gas station and spoke up before the silence could become all-consuming.

"Let me out here. Pull in like you're gonna go get gas. I'll go inside, and you leave me."

She nodded and drove into the station. A battered Pete's Gas with the last number missing on the diesel price. She pulled to a stop in front of pump number four and put the car into park.

"Guess this is it. Be careful, okay?" she said, and before I could reply, she got out to pump gas.

"I will," I mumbled, getting out myself. I nodded to her and made like I was going inside to pay.

Once inside, I took a moment to steady myself. I had exactly zero plan here, and that was bad. The only reason I'd been able to take out Elliott was because of the plan the three of us had hatched at the diner.

This? This felt insane, and worse, the longer we waited, the more likely Jimmy would vanish. No. I had to do this now and hope for the best. And God how I hated hoping for the best…

When I got back outside, the Florida humidity hit me like a sloppy kiss. I ignored it and watched Mary Ann pull her car back into the street, leaving me behind. As she merged back into traffic, I let out a little breath of relief. One of us might survive this.

CHAPTER 20

The red façade of Terrific Tom's surprised me as I approached. I hadn't noticed it before, but the lights that lit up the letters in the name were out, and the windows had that dusty, never been washed look. The sign on the door read closed for renovations, but judging by the inch of grime settled around said sign, this place had never opened. I took a quick glance around the lot and sighed.

Terrific Tom's reminded me of an old Thai food restaurant I'd seen back in Ventura. I'd never ever seen anyone eat there, and the one time I'd ventured inside, I'd been informed by a tank-top wearing Asian covered in tattoos that the place was closed despite it being 12 PM on a Saturday.

I'd later learned the place was a front for

laundering money by some gang with a name I couldn't pronounce. Or at least, that's what the local news had told me.

Terrific Tom's gave off the same vibe, and as I crossed the pavement in front of it to look around, I wondered if anyone was even here. I mean, there were only a couple scattered vehicles in the lot, and most of them seemed to be in front of the Pawn Pros pawnshop.

Still, I was here, might as well check it out. I began walking, intending to circle the building, but as I passed by the glass double doors, I caught sight of a shadow inside. I turned toward it just in time for a bullet to pass by my ear. Glass shattered inward into the building as I dropped to my belly and rolled. Another bullet ricocheted off the cement beside me as I came up on my feet, drawing my Glock and looking for a target. Off by the street, a beat up golden Ford Fiesta tore ass away down the street.

Had that been another hitter? Worse, how did they know I was here?

I wasn't sure, but before I could reach into my pocket to warn Mary Ann about the attack, Terrific Tom's came alive like a kicked anthill. Two bare-chested thugs with meth-ruined teeth appeared in the broken window and raised submachine guns in my general direction. Their bullets cut an erratic line through the broken window in front of me before spitting off into the distance while I threw myself to the side and fired.

Four quick shots took the two guys down because, evidently, they didn't know about cover. Before their friends who had smartly dropped out of sight could fire at me, I sprinted toward the corner of the building.

The side of the building held no windows or doors, and I breathed a sigh of relief. Adrenaline surged through my veins, and as panic swam into my gut, I pushed it down because I had no need of it now. Instead, I focused on the gun in my hand as the sound of the front doors opening filled my ears.

Boot steps crunching on broken glass.

The odd squeak of a heel on cement.

The sudden stop as someone approached the corner.

I crouched down low and waited. The thug came around, shotgun raised to blow me away if I'd been standing. Because I was low, his shot passed over my head. I dropped him with two quick shots to the chest. He fell backward in a spray of blood as I whirled in time to see two more guys coming around the backside of the building.

Another set of shots dropped them, and as I stood there, chest heaving, I wondered who had trained these guys. They might be tough, but they were thug tough, not ex-military tough. These were little more than skinhead punks who thought holding a piece made them tough. They weren't. Not by my standards.

I sprinted toward the back end of the building. As I approached the two men I'd shot, I did a quick sweep of the back alley. There was no one there, so I quickly holstered my own Glock and grabbed the SMGs the two had been holding. The damned things didn't even have stocks. No wonder they had been so inaccurate.

Still, they'd make a lot of noise and could cause a lot of damage in enclosed spaces, which if I had to guess, Terrific Tom's was full of. I moved toward the back doors, still half open from when the pair had come out and let loose a blast of gunfire. Bullets cut an upward arc through the cheap metal and the wall to the left. I moved forward, dropping the left gun to hang on my shoulder by its strap as I grabbed the edge of the door.

I maneuvered to the side and pulled it open and toward me while staying next to the wall so I wouldn't get perforated. To my surprise, no gunfire followed the door as it opened, and I stood there in silence, my ears ringing.

I slowly crept out from behind the door and grabbed my cell phone, switched it to camera mode and crouched down. Then I held it out, allowing the camera to show me the inside without having to poke my head around the edge. No one appeared in the screen. Hell, I could see all the way to a counter a few meters away, and there was no trace of anyone.

A breath of relief escaped me as I pocketed my phone, hoisted both SMGs and moved into the threshold, crouched down low.

I took a few quick steps forward. As I reached the counter, I realized I was in the kitchen. There were no utensils or pots and pans, but it was a kitchen nonetheless.

Interesting.

I glanced down a hallway to the left, surmising it led back to the main area. I could hear men shuffling around that way, but they were probably trying to figure out where I'd gone, but at the same time, they had to know because I had been letting off blasts from the stolen SMGs. Maybe they thought it was their friends.

Either way, I had to be quick. It was hard because the only light in the room came from a dusty skylight overhead. No electric lights had been turned on inside the place.

After a few more seconds of searching, I realized the only way out was through the hallway and toward the gunmen. Maybe that's why they hadn't come?

I moved slowly down it, and as I did, I heard the nervous movements of untrained men. Still, I was hoping to avoid them if I could. Untrained or not, a bullet will kill you dead the same either way.

As I headed toward a big pair of arches dug into the left wall that led into the main room, I spied another door just before it with the words "Staff Only" written across it in black lettering. At the end of the hallway were two more doors with restroom placards.

Easy choice.

I pulled up short of the archway and grabbed the handle of the staff door. It was locked. I could blow it open, but that would alert the thugs in the other room. That left one last place to go.

Crouching down once more, I edged toward the arches and peeked out. There were four thugs. Three with shotguns and one with a pistol. None of them were looking back here, at least not yet. I sighted the SMGs on the thugs and let loose.

It was over before I finished exhaling. The four bodies hit the ground in a spray of blood and bone, and as they lay there, fluid leaking out of them, I realized they'd brought the bodies of their dead comrades inside.

"So that's what you guys did instead of coming to find me," I muttered. They'd wanted to hide the bodies. Guess it didn't matter much. I was gonna take them down piece by piece until I found my dad, no matter what.

Satisfied there were no more thugs in the vicinity, I whirled and kicked the staff door as hard as I could. The lock broke through the jamb as the door swung inward and smacked against the wall. The room inside was empty. How could that be?

Jimmy was supposed to be here, dammit.

I turned, and as I did, a shotgun blast nearly took my goddamned head off. It cleaved through the drywall to the left of my head as I fired the SMGs at my unseen opponent.

Bullets ripped through the wall as the two guns ran empty. That's when I saw a glint by the counter in the kitchen. Someone was smart and using cover, and worse, I had none.

I dove into the room, dropping the spent SMGs as another shotgun blast came down the hallway. As I landed hard on my side and pain shot up my elbow, I pulled my Glock and counted to three.

"You're dead! You hear me?" a shrill, angry voice cried from the hallway beyond.

"Look, buddy. I'm looking for Jimmy," I called back, creeping toward the doorway and trying to decide how best to take him without getting shot. "Tell me where he is, and I won't kill you. Look around. I'm a lot better at it than you."

"Jimmy's not here, man! He left for a meeting," the thug said, his voice cracking. "You'll pay for this!" I heard footsteps retreating. Was he running?

I peeked out and saw nothing, so I moved forward. As I reached the kitchen, I heard the back door slam shut.

Damn.

I got to my feet and raced outside after him. The sunlight was practically blinding after being inside, but I ignored it as I scanned the horizon for the perp.

"Where did you go?" I asked aloud as I stepped into the parking lot, looking for him. Had he escaped into the pawnshop?

The rest of my thoughts were cut off as a car slammed into me from behind, taking my legs out from under me and throwing me to the pavement. My world went blurry as I slammed into the hard ground and lay there trying to remember how to breathe.

Before I could do even that, arms grabbed my arms and legs and hauled me into the air. My body was slammed down on the hood of the black Dodge SUV.

While I was held there, my brain still rattling around in my skull, a guy wearing a wife beater and a black leather jacket with a silver scorpion emblazoned across it moved toward me. His left hand held one of those butterfly knives, and as he flipped it around, bringing the glinting blade into the air, my breath caught in my throat. I struggled, trying to throw the arms holding me off, but it was no use.

"You thought you were so smart, didn't you. Well, old Troy's got a few tricks up his sleeve. Go ahead and struggle, you've got lots of people to pay for," the Scorpion said as the men holding me spread my legs. "You've got balls, and I like that." His face curled into a devious smirk. "I think I'll have to do something about that." He smashed the hood between my legs with one hand. "Now hold still. This is gonna hurt you a lot more than it hurts me."

As he raised the knife to cut off my junk, police sirens cut through the air. The guy's knife disappeared in a flash, and he stepped back, rage filling his features as a brown sedan rolled up.

A black guy with one of those bulldog faces leaned out the window and gave the group of us a once over. As it happened, the four guys holding me down let up, hauling me to my feet and dusting me off.

"Is there a problem here?" the black guy asked in a syrupy sweet drawl, his badge glinting in the light as his partner, a white guy with shaggy brown hair and blue eyes, watched from the passenger seat. "Because I'd hate if there was a problem, Troy."

"No problem," Troy said, gesturing at me. "Buddy just fell, and we were helping him up."

"You're full of crap," the cop deadpanned as the siren cut off. "Now get out of here." He made a shooing gesture with his hands.

"Otherwise I might want to talk to you."

Troy glared at the cop before biting his lip and nodding. "Suit yourself, officer." Then he, along with the rest of the Scorpions, piled into their SUV, started it with a roar of engines, and took off down the alley.

The cop watched them go before turning his dour eyes on me. "You need to get in the car now." He gestured to the backseat.

"Excuse me?" I asked, rubbing my neck as I tried to ignore the pain coursing through my body. I really didn't have time for this, but what else was I supposed to do? Run from the cops?

"Look, you're Bob Ryder's kid. We know he's missing and that you just showed up." He nodded toward the Terrific Tom's. "Doesn't take a genius to see what you're up to." My heart started to pound, and I took half a step backward, only as I did, the guy's partner clapped his hand on the handle of his door, while waving his other one.

"He's gonna run, Cam." As he spoke, I readied myself to do just that. If I got arrested, there'd be no one to save my dad.

"Don't run," the Cam said, shaking his head. "If you do, we'll have to chase you, except I'm old and hate running, so I'll just put a bullet in your leg." He shifted so I could see his Dirty Harry revolver. "Then there will be paperwork, and I do not want that."

"Yeah, we really hate paperwork," his partner agreed.

"What do you want?" I asked, raising an eyebrow at the cop.

"What we said earlier, Billy," the partner in the passenger seat said. "To talk." He jerked a thumb toward the back of the sedan. "So get in."

I nodded. "If this is where you drive me to the middle of nowhere to kill me, you're going to have another thing coming," I said as I got into the car. It was surprisingly clean and didn't smell like coffee or cigarettes. Instead, the smell of carwash pine trees filled the air.

"Buddy, if we wanted you dead, we wouldn't have interrupted Troy and his boys. They're a bunch of screw-ups, but they'd get the job done well enough." Cam's eyes fixed me in the rearview mirror. "No. What you've done is make a three-year investigation go sideways."

CHAPTER 21

As we pulled into a parking garage several blocks away, I still wasn't quite sure if they were going to try and kill me or not. The entire ride had passed with them making inane small talk with each other about pool while completely ignoring my questions. Worse, I'd managed to lose my Glock when Troy had jumped me. If it came down to a fight, I was outmatched.

The one time they had spoken to me had been to tell me to wait. Still, they hadn't taken my phone, and I'd let Mary Ann know what was going on. She knew the parking structure and would be here in no time.

"Thank you for your patience," the cop in the passenger seat, a fella named Doug, said as he turned around and stared at me with his baby blue peepers. I got the feeling they saw a lot more than they let on. "But you have to understand, the discussion we're about to have is, well, not something for everyone's ears."

"Okay..." I said, letting the word trail off as we pulled into a parking spot beside the stairwell on the third floor.

"Come on out, and leave your phone in the backseat. If you have a watch, leave that too. I don't want you recording us," Cam said, throwing the sedan into park before tossing his own phone and radio on the seat. Beside him, Doug did the same, and the two of them stepped out of the vehicle to wait for me.

I sighed and dug my phone out of my pocket before tossing it on the seat. Then I pulled off my old dive watch and stared at it for a moment. It was a silver Grovana Men's Diver Watch and had set me back about five hundred bucks when I'd purchased it. I wasn't even sure why I'd wanted it, other than I felt like I should have a nice watch that could also withstand some water.

"You coming?" Cam asked, his drawl filling my ears as he watched me set the watch down on the seat and get out. "Because if you were under the illusion that my partner's time is not valuable, I would have you know that is one-hundred-percent true." He touched his chest with one finger. "My time, on the other hand, is quite valuable."

"Sorry," I said, shutting the door and moving toward them. "It's been a long day."

"S'okay," Doug replied and began walking. "Let's go."

Not knowing what the hell was going on, I had no choice but to follow the two cops as we made our way up the stairs to the fifth floor of the six-level structure. They stopped in the stairwell in front of the battered metal door with a giant five spray painted on it.

"So here's the deal," Cam said, shoving his hands in his pockets. The movement caused his cheap suit jacket to open, revealing his Glock tucked away in its holster. "We know everything."

"Everything?" I asked, raising an eyebrow and trying to play off the statement even though I was pretty sure I was about to go to jail forever.

"Yes," Cam said, shooting me a knowing smile. "That's why we're here. We like what you've been doing."

"Say again?" I said, taking a deep breath. It felt like I'd just been sucker punched, but not in a bad way. More like when you're sitting in class, and some cute girl slides a note on your desk that says "I like you…"

"See, here's the thing," Doug said, edging close enough for me to smell the eggs he'd eaten for breakfast. "The top brass down at the precinct is crooked." He held up a hand. "The

DA, the mayor, anyone who matters or gets elected? They work for the Scorpions. That's why when your house got shot up in broad daylight, no one came."

As his explanation settled over me, I got angrier. I'd been going after these guys because I was trying to find my dad. I hadn't realized just how much of a cancer the Scorpions had become. Worse, that cancer had been spreading, and no one, save my dad, had done a goddamned thing to stop it.

"No one can touch the Scorpions," Cam added, sighing as the weight of years of injustice settled over him. "Until you came and went to town on their asses. Now we've got two leaders dead, and the ants are scrambling. Now is when it gets worse." He wiped his brow. "Hopefully, it gets better after."

"Worse?" I asked, confusion filling me. So they knew what I'd done, but I was still here. How was that possible? "What do you mean by worse?"

"There's a Fed who has been in deep cover for years. He's up there in the Scorpions now. We've never met him, but he dropped your name to us. Said they'd make a play for you." Doug sighed. "That is something my partner and I do not want to see happen. It's why we tailed you to Troy's place, and believe me, if we did, they did too."

A snake of panic slithered up from my gut

at their words.

"Wait does that mean Mary Ann—"

"No." He cut me off. "She'll be fine. My friend is watching her. He's clean as a whistle. You have some time. Not a lot, but some."

"Why are they making a play for me?" I asked, thanking my lucky stars she was okay. If anything happened to her, it'd be one hundred percent my fault, and I'd have a hard time living with that. "I mean, more than the obvious."

"You killed two big shots in the organization. They can't let that stand or the locals might get uppity." Cam cracked a smile at me. "The big boss wants to personally see you." Cam drew a thumb across his throat. "This will be your one chance to take the head guy out. Do that, and the Scorpions will degenerate into infighting. The mayor and the DA will start burning them to keep their careers from going under. Everyone will be better for it."

"I'm not interested in that," I said, waving my hand and glancing back to the car. I wanted to call Mary Ann and make sure she was okay. Part of me was just glad she was on her way here. "I'm not some kind of action hero. I'm just trying to get my dad back."

"Fortunately, our asset has a line on your dad. He says that as soon as you do this, he'll turn over all his information to you." Cam smiled, showing his teeth, and while it was supposed to be reassuring, it was anything but. "Now does that sound like a deal or does that sound like a deal?"

"Whoa," I said, trying to keep the tears from filling my eyes as the lump in my throat got twice as large. "You mean he's alive? My dad, I mean. Part of me had thought..."

"For now, but I got the impression that was subject to change," Doug said, putting a hand on my shoulder, but I almost didn't see it because I was suddenly so happy I could have screamed. Tears threatened to cloud my vision as I turned to look at the man.

"Thank you," I whispered, swallowing hard. He was alive. Thank God. It meant I could still save him, that there was still time. Now, I needed to hurry more than ever.

"Don't thank me. It won't be long before said Head of Scorpions leaks your name to the police, pinpointing you as a homegrown terrorist. So, you need to finish this fast because once that happens, we really won't be able to help you." He shrugged. "You're in too deep. This only ends one of two ways for you, now."

I screwed up my face with my hands. On the one hand, my dad was alive. On the other, they'd really given me nothing I didn't know. Worse, I had no way of knowing where this boss was, or how to get to him. Somehow I had to make all that work so I could take out the leader of the criminal organization that owned this entire city.

"How do you expect me to do that?" I asked, wiping my eyes with the back of one hand. "I don't even know who runs the Scorpions."

"We don't either, but we do know his boat, the Hard Tide, is coming in tonight. There was supposed to be a meeting between the heads of the organization. It's locked down tighter than a drum, but if you can get in there, you have a real shot at taking him and all his people out in one fell swoop." Cam gave me a reassuring smile that did anything but. He was serious.

"So let me get this straight. You expect me to somehow get onto a boat filled with gang members and kill them all? By myself?" I asked, incredulous. "Because that sounds insane."

"I didn't say it would be easy," Cam replied and threw his hands in the air in front of himself. "But what choice do you have." He glanced at his wrist where his watch would have been and frowned. "I'm guessing you have, at most, six hours before we get the order to actually bring you in. Once that happens, you're screwed."

"Thanks for telling me," I mumbled, casting my gaze skyward. It was insane, but I had to try. I hadn't come down here to lie low. No, I'd come here to find my dad, and since finding Jimmy hadn't worked out, it was time to focus on the Hard Tide.

"Sorry we can't help more, but it wouldn't be wise. We'd draw attention, and that would just wind up ruining your window of opportunity," Doug said, slapping me on the shoulder. "We'll do our best to run interference, though."

"Thanks," I said, hoping that would be worth a damn but knowing it probably wouldn't be. These guys had gone out on a limb just talking to me, and what's worse, Troy would know it. That meant something, but I wasn't sure how much.

Still, I wanted to find my dad, and if that meant I had to take down a drug cartel, then I was taking down a drug cartel. First things first though, I had to get back in the game, and that meant meeting up with Mary Ann and Ren to formulate a plan.

"You're welcome," the cops said in unison. They looked at each other for a second. An uneasy laughter broke out between them before fading into the emptiness of the stairwell.

"Good luck," Cam said, holding his hand out to me.

"Thanks," I said, shaking his hand. His grip was firm but not bone-crushingly strong.

"Now let's get you your stuff back so you

can get on your way." Doug nodded down the stairs behind me. "Hope you didn't mind the hike too much."

CHAPTER 22

"Well, that was interesting," I said as I flopped down in the passenger seat of Mary Ann's car and let out a slow breath. My dad was alive, and what's more, I had a way to find him. That meant I would find him.

"Penny for your thoughts?" she asked as Cam and Doug left the parking lot, moving past our position without a backward glance.

"Turns out dad might actually be alive," I told her.

Relief washed over her features. "That's great! Did they know where he is?" she asked, excitement tingeing her words.

"You remember that boat Ren talked about?" I asked, pulling out my phone.

"The Hard Tide?" She chewed on her lips. "What about it?"

"Turns out the Scorpions' head honcho is on the boat and is holding some kind of meeting. Seems there's an undercover agent who knows about dad but won't give me the info unless I do something about said meeting."

"Do something?" she asked, one hand tightening around the wheel as she threw the car into reverse and backed out of the space. "What are you supposed to do?"

"What I've been doing, but bigger." I sighed and stared at the ceiling of the car. "Can't say those cats don't deserve it."

"That's suicide, Billy." She swallowed and looked over at me. "I think it is high time you called the police—"

"Those were the police, Mary Ann. They can't help. This whole town is locked up tighter than a cookie jar at dinner time." I rubbed my face with my hands. "I don't think there's another way." As I spoke, I scrolled to Ren's number in my phone and hit call.

"You don't know that," Mary Ann said as Ren answered.

"I do," I said, glancing at the phone. "Hey, Ren, we just got a tip that the Hard Tide is supposed to be holding some kind of meeting. When's it at, and how the hell do I get into it?"

"Midnight, and you don't," Ren replied, his voice distracted. "I'm looking at the invite right here..." He paused for a moment, and I heard keys tapping in the background. "Wait, that's it."

"What do you mean?" I asked, my heart lifting slightly. Had he found something that would let us sneak into the meeting?

"The invites are encrypted, but I can get past that." He paused once more, and I could see him gesturing at the screen in his mind's eye. "Sorry, I was pointing at the computer. Anyway, long story short, I can get you through the security if you can get out to the boat."

"Explain in more detail?" I asked as Mary Ann gave me a look that let me know we'd have words when I hung up. Damn. I had hoped to avoid that.

"Basically the invite has a passcode that you can load onto an id card to identify yourself to security and open doors. I can crack it for you, but obviously, I can't hack you onto a boat a couple miles out to sea if you catch my drift." Ren sighed loudly. "If I was closer, I could do it. At least, I think I can. It will depend on if they have deactivated Jack's code. If they've done that, you're probably going to catch a few extra holes in the head, if you know what I mean."

"Sounds like a fool proof plan if there ever was," I muttered. "Let me know when you're ready to try."

"Will do," he replied as I hung up. Mary Ann glared at me even though she was in traffic. I cringed.

"Please tell me you're not going through with this," she said, voice hard and angry.

"What do you mean?" I asked, narrowing my eyes at her, but if it bothered her, she didn't show it. "Of course I'm going through with it. There's no other way."

"I heard Ren. That boat is out in the middle of the ocean. That means we need to sail to it." She waved one hand to the left, indicating the darkening sky outside. "We can take your dad's boat, but you can't sail alone at night. For one that's suicide, and for two, you haven't sailed in how long?"

"Since mom died," I said, swallowing hard as I shut my eyes, recalling the memory of my Dad and me spreading her ashes in the Channel Islands out in California. It'd been where my mom and dad had met forever and a half ago. She'd told him he needed a bigger boat, and he'd known on the spot he needed to marry her.

"Exactly, so you'll need help, and if you recall, I used to be pretty good at the whole sailing thing." I let her words rattle around in my head as we moved along the busy street. "And where are we going?"

"To the docks," I said, hoping there wouldn't be a welcome committee waiting for us there.

Assuming we got to the boat intact, she was

right. I did need help. If the weather was at all bad, it'd be really hard for me to adjust the sails on dad's Catalina 36 and steer by myself.

If the conditions were bad, sailing by yourself had a lot more luck to it than I cared to admit, and being that I was rusty and was going to infiltrate the Hard Tide at the end of it, the absolute last thing I wanted to do was get killed on the way. That'd save no one.

If I was being honest with myself, I'd realize I needed her with me. Only I was being pig-headed and wanting to keep her safe. Which was why I'd left her without a word so many years ago because, at the end of the day, I didn't want her married to a soldier who might not come back.

This time was no different, and while I was willing to take an inordinate amount of risk myself, I needed her to come with me if I had any hope of pulling it off, if only just to keep the boat in a place where I could get back to it after the job was done. She had to come whether I liked it or not.

"Okay," I whispered as we pulled in front of the docks. The police had long since cleared out, but they were still funneling people through the side entrance.

"Okay, what?" she asked, moving her car into line.

"Okay, you can come sailing with me," I replied before gesturing at the line of cars.

"You know, assuming we ever get inside."

CHAPTER 23

"Your friend is here," Mary Ann called as I rummaged alone in the cabin of the Catalina 36, trying to make sure everything was situated correctly. Honestly, I wasn't quite sure. While I'd helped my dad get the boat ready, it'd been almost twenty years ago, and what's more, most of his instruction hadn't been explanatory. It'd been more, "Boy, grab that line," or "Boy, turn that knob."

"Okay," I said, looking around one last time. It felt like I was forgetting something, but I wasn't sure what. Unsatisfied, I climbed back out and found Mary Ann messing with the rigging on top of the boat. I wasn't quite sure what she was checking because both the mainsail and the headsail were strapped down, and we wouldn't be using either until we motored out of the harbor.

"Hey, help me with this stuff," Ren called from the dock, and I swung my gaze toward him. He was standing there dressed in a sweatshirt and blue jeans and a fishing hat. His nose was covered by a smear of white zinc sunscreen as were the tops of his ears. Beside his feet was a backpack and another bag about the size of a large suitcase. He looked me over warily and shifted his garment bag over one shoulder.

"So much stuff?" I asked, climbing up onto the side of the boat and stepping across the water to the staircase on the side of the dock. I took the three steps down and looked at all his stuff. "Do you really need all that?"

"Me? No. But you will." He shot me a grin before shoving the garment bag into my hands. "That's a suit. It should fit."

"A suit?" I asked, raising an eyebrow as he grabbed his backpack in one hand and hoisted it onto one shoulder. Then he stepped past me and moved up the stairs.

"Yes, a suit," he affirmed as he stared dubiously at the chasm between the boat and the dock. He stepped across it, one hand snaking out to grab the stainless steel pole next to the safety wires. He hoisted himself on board and hopped down into the cockpit of the boat.

"What do I need a suit for?" I asked,

grabbing the bag he'd left on the dock.

It was heavy as all get out. Hoisting the strap onto my shoulder, I made my way to the boat and looked at him.

"For infiltrating the party?" He gestured at me as I tossed the bag onto the deck before stepping aboard myself. "You'll stick out like a sore thumb like that."

"Excellent point, but how the hell do you expect me to get there in any kind of shape to do that?" I grabbed onto the wooden handle attached to the boat to steady myself before stepping down inside. I dropped the garment bag on the bench before turning to grab the heavier bag.

"Hence the dry suit." He pointed to the heavy bag as I lugged it onto the seat.

"You can't be serious," I muttered, glancing down at the bag. Then I very slowly unzipped it to find myself staring at a metal tank. No wonder the thing had been so damned heavy. Full tanks weighed something like thirty-five pounds on their own.

"Look, I know you hate scuba diving since we did it down in Peru that one time," Ren said, flopping down on the seat and hauling a laptop out of his backpack. "But I figure it like this. Our best bet is for you to put on the suit and scuba your ass over to the boat. Then you can climb aboard, shed the gear, and be all done up in your suit." He nodded like it was a great plan.

"And what if I get wet anyway?" I asked, raising an eyebrow at him.

"Then you're back at square one," he replied, shrugging. "So you may as well try."

"I suppose," I muttered, rubbing my chin in thought. "Did you get the other stuff I asked about?"

"The C4 and the guns? Yeah, they're in the waterproof bag at the bottom. They weren't cheap, and you owe me. It was why this took so long." He waved a hand at the darkening horizon as the wind blew by. "We have time, but not much. We'll definitely need to hurry."

"Roger," I said, taking the two bags down the steps and tossing them in the small alcove behind the desk. Then I grabbed a life jacket and brought it back upstairs with me. "Put this on." I held it out to Ren.

"I don't really do life jackets." He wrinkled his nose. "The way I figure it is if I fall in, that will just prolong the agony."

"Look, buddy, if you wear the jacket, I'll come back and get you." I shook the jacket at him. "At least give me a fighting chance to do it."

He thought about it for a moment and nodded. "Fair enough." He took the jacket from me and put it on. "What's the whistle for?" He fingered the orange whistle tied to one of the straps.

"It's so that when you fall in and get tired of screaming for help, you can still make noise." I shot him a hard look before turning to look at Mary Ann. "Tell him."

"Billy's right." She adjusted something else on the jib before hopping down and coming toward me.

"Fine," Ren said, rolling his eyes and putting up his hands. "I get it."

"I think we're ready," Mary Ann said, waving a hand at the rigging. "Well, based on what I remember. I haven't been on the Storm Ryder in a year."

"You went on it that recently?" I asked, somewhat surprised.

"Yeah, your dad was teaching me to sail, but I ran out of money to pay him for lessons." She fidgeted. "He didn't ask for money, but I felt bad making him do it for free."

"He probably liked the company," I said, feeling guilty because my dad had been trying to get me to come out and sail with him for a couple years, and I hadn't because I hadn't wanted to see Mary Ann. Not after what I'd done to her. Too scared and stupid.

"Now don't you go feeling bad," she said, moving beside me and touching my arm with one delicate finger. "I know that look, and let me just say, I'm glad you're back." She smiled at me, and it made her eyes sparkle like the ocean around us.

"Yes, ma'am," I said as the sun started to set, casting hues of gold, purple, and aqua across the horizon. "You wanna steer?"

"Why don't you do it for now? We can trade when the sails need to go up." She flopped down opposite Ren. "Or are you under the impression I got on this boat to work harder than I absolutely had to?"

"You make an excellent point." I nodded.

"Besides, we all know the first thirty-six feet and the last thirty-six feet of any sail is the most dangerous. You trying to pawn that off on me, Billy Ryder?" she asked, raising a shapely eyebrow at me.

"I wouldn't dream of it." I made my way behind the steering wheel, knelt down, and made sure the kill key was pushed in. Then I turned the key to the on position and hit the second button from the right. The ship roared to life, and as it did, I turned to look out the back. My heart sank.

"No water coming out the back," I muttered, scratching my head as I tried in vain to think of what might have gone wrong. I hastily turned back to the engine and pulled the pull key, causing the boat to shut off. I didn't want to risk the engine burning up when water wasn't cycling through.

"Did you check the thru-hull? I remember your dad always keeping them closed," Mary Ann offered, and as she spoke, I felt my cheeks heat up. She was right, of course, and I hadn't even checked.

"You're a genius," I said, moving past her and going to the valve. I opened it and smirked. I'd grabbed the key right off the top of the valve and forgotten to open it. If it'd been my boat, I'd have deserved to burn up the engine.

"I know," she said as I returned and moved back to start the boat. This time when I pressed the button, water did come out the backside. I glanced around, making sure there were no lines still attached to the dock. Once satisfied I was okay, I began to pull out into the water.

"Say, what are the coordinates for the Hard Tide?" I asked, glancing at Ren. "I wanna put them in the GPS."

"Not gonna use a chart?" He gestured at the boat. "I hear that's what sailors do."

"No. They're downstairs for one and covered in coffee and beer stains. And besides, I want something actively tracking our target."

"I was just messing with you." He glanced at his screen for a moment, before looking up at me and telling me the coordinates which I punched into the onboard Garmin GPS.

It was a few miles away and wouldn't take too long to reach. Even still, I could tell by the way the sun was dipping into the horizon, it'd be dark well before we arrived. Hopefully, that'd be to our advantage.

CHAPTER 24

Even though the Hard Tide was in the direction of the damned wind, we were still making good time since I'd managed to keep us at a close-reach for most of the time. Or at least we were making good time because with about a mile until we needed to switch over the headsail and tack, the wind died down to nothing. As I stared at the luffing sails while trying desperately to turn the boat to keep them full, I knew it was pointless.

"Damn," I muttered, gesturing at the sails. "No wind."

"So why don't you just turn on the motor and keep going?" Ren asked as I bent down to do just that.

"That's not the problem," Mary Ann said, sitting a little straighter in her seat and looking

170

up at me with a concerned expression.

"What's the problem then?" Ren followed her gaze, confusion on his face. "I don't see anything. Clouds are too thick."

"The problem is that when the wind dies like that, it usually means we're about to get bad weather real soon. Normally, any sailor would turn back now." I sighed as the motor started. I got back up to continue toward our destination. "Something, we can't afford to do."

"How do you know?" Ren asked, clutching his laptop tightly to his chest.

"I suggest you put that away downstairs if you want to keep it," Mary Ann said, waving a hand at the computer. "Because things are about to get a lot worse."

Ren nodded, doing as she said as I threw the throttle forward, sending the Storm Ryder leaping over the waves. Even though it was dark, I could tell from the way the white foam on the crests of the long waves was blowing off that we were somewhere around a six on the Beaufort scale. If it was going to get worse, that would mean we'd be in full gale-force conditions. Damn.

It happened without warning about half a mile later. The wind picked up, slamming into the sails and sending us rocketing forward at nearly ten knots. It was crazy because we'd been doing about five and a half with the motor, which had felt fast until the wind had picked up.

Waves crested all around us, throwing spray across the front of the boat as I did my best to keep us on target. The wheel fought beneath my hands as Mary Ann scurried up toward the rigging for the mainsail, trying to adjust it.

"You wanna switch?" I cried over the wind and waves as we came down off the crest of a wave to slam down into the water. As the impact thudded up through my belly, the wave we'd come over crashed down into the back of the boat, soaking me to the bone in salty water. My eyes went wide as a rush of cold went over me, and even if I hadn't been awake, I was now.

"Are these kinds of waves normal?" Ren asked right before we lurched up over a wave, and his face turned green. His cheeks bulged like a chipmunk as he spun in his seat, thrust his head toward the safety wire, and puked all over the side of the damned boat.

"No. This is abnormally bad," Mary Ann said, moving across the distance between them and rubbing his back. "It's okay, Ren. There are only two kinds of sailors anyway. The one's who have been seasick, and the ones who are going to be seasick."

Ren didn't respond because he was too busy vomiting.

"Man, I actually feel bad for bringing you now," I said, fighting against the wheel as another wave sent us slamming back into the sea. It was pissing me off because if it was daytime, I'd have been able to see the waves and would have been less subject to the sea's whims.

"Not as bad as I feel," Ren replied as the sea kicked up again, forcing the boat damned near up on its side. I braced my feet against the corner of the boat, fighting to stay upright while Mary Ann grabbed onto one of the handles for support. I really hoped no one fell out now because if someone did, it'd be hard as hell to get them back.

The sails whipped as we came back down, and I turned the boat hard to the left in an effort to keep out of the no-sail zone. As I got the Storm Ryder back under control, another wave came up over the bow, spraying me with saltwater moments before we went back up on our side. The main sail practically touched the ocean as I fought for control again.

"If you get tired, I can take over for a bit," Mary Ann said, shooting a dubious glance at Ren. "Since I doubt your buddy can take over."

I nodded, glancing at the Garmin. We still had about twenty minutes to our target, partially because we were now doing almost eleven knots. "I think I've got about twenty more minutes in me before I need to rest."

"Is that what it says on there?" she asked as we went practically horizontal again, and I dug my foot into the corner, causing the sea water that spilled inside to soak through my sneaker. Honestly, I wasn't even sure the boat could handle it, and we'd be really screwed if the mast just ripped out of the boat from the wind.

"Yep," I replied as we came back down, and I was treated to water running off the end of the bench behind me and down the back of my legs.

"Then you should let me take over. You need to get all that scuba gear on, and we won't be able to circle well like this." She started moving toward me, keeping her hand on the railing as she did so. "Besides, you're going to have to make a negative descent because of the conditions." She shook her head. "I do not envy you. Night diving is bad enough."

"Yeah, I hate night dives too. It's worse because you know there are sharks down there who can see a whole hell of a lot better than you can." I nodded as she grabbed the wheel, stabilizing it.

As I let go and tried to make my way toward the cabin, the boat went up on its side, and I reached out, grabbing onto the steel for support. As we crashed back down and spray hit me in the face, I turned back to Mary Ann. "I want you both to tether in." I jerked a thumb at Ren. "Him especially."

Ren threw up by way of response.

"Okay," Mary Ann said, reaching into the cubby beside the starter and pulling out a tether. She hooked one end to her jacket and the other to the railing. Then she tossed another to me. I caught it and got Ren all hooked in.

Satisfied, I headed below. It was hard as hell to stay stable because the boat kept rocking like a son of a gun, but I did my best to pull my ass into the suit I'd been given. It made me feel a little ridiculous, but I ignored it because Ren was right. If I was going to be infiltrating a party full of thugs in three-piece suits, I should try to blend in.

I sat down on the bench and pulled on a pair of sweat-wicking socks before pulling the dry suit on and was immediately happy it had dry socks already attached. Ren had thought of everything. A couple minutes later, I was all zipped up and had tightened the straps around the gloves and booties.

Satisfied I wasn't going to get my suit wet unless I sprung a leak, I got back on my feet and pulled the hood out of the bag before pulling it on. It took a minute to get it adjusted, but once it was, I was burning up. It was always crazy to me how quickly the temperature went from tolerable to intolerable when I had full scuba gear on.

Still, I was nearly ready to get in the water. I grabbed the waterproof bag containing the C4, keycard, and Glock from the scuba bag and attached it to the dangle on my hip. I checked it to make sure there were no obvious holes, then I grabbed the aluminum tank and hauled it out. A quick turn of the knob let me know there was air inside. Hopefully, it'd be enough to get me there.

I took a moment to get it out onto the deck and cursed as the boat rocked, throwing me into the bench.

"You should have stuck it in the rack before we got underway," Mary Ann said, muscles straining as she fought against the wheel. All around me foam was spraying, and if it hadn't been for my dry suit, I'd have been soaked as water splashed me. Damn. We were likely going to have to close the doors to the cabin to keep from getting water inside and sinking the old girl.

"I know," I snapped, more angry at myself than her as I wrestled the air tank into the rack and pulled the Velcro strap tight. "But you know the thing about hindsight being twenty, twenty."

"Don't you snap at me because you're mad at yourself, Billy Rider," Mary Ann said as she spun the wheel, allowing us to take a wave at an angle. Even still, the front of the boat was nearly buried beneath the water.

"Sorry, ma'am. Won't happen again," I replied before going down below and grabbing my fins and mask. I headed back up, and as I got to the top, I pulled the doors shut and secured them with the lock to keep them from opening.

"See that it doesn't," she replied as I pulled my fins on. I always hated walking around the boat in fins, but there was no way I'd be able to put them on in the water. Not with it being this rough and me having to do a negative-buoyancy entry.

Despite all the tossing of the seas, I had the air tank strapped in and ready to go a moment later, and as I sat there watching the surf, I spotted a bright green beacon in the distance.

"Is that it?" I asked, pointing.

Ren gave me a sickly nod. "Yeah. I think so. I remember reading about the beacon."

"I feel like you should have pointed that out earlier," Mary Ann said, and as Ren raised one hand to reply, the boat lurched. He threw himself back toward the edge as his stomach emptied more of its contents over the side.

"I find it hard to believe you have anything left inside you," I said as I donned my mask and prepared to enter.

"I do too," he mumbled as we came closer, and I noticed other boats all around. We were close now, and if we got much closer, they might spot us.

"Here's good. We're at least a quarter mile off," I said, climbing up on the side. "I don't want you two getting too close."

"Be careful, Billy," Mary Ann said, and I nodded back at her.

"I will," I said right before I stepped off the edge of a perfectly good boat and fell into the water on purpose.

CHAPTER 25

As I hit the water and plunged through the churning waves and into the ocean's depths, I marveled at how quickly the temperature changed. I'd scuba dived a bunch of times, and every single time it amazed me how quickly I went from sweating like a pig, to comfortable, to downright chilly.

Fortunately, I was in Florida, so the water was quite a bit warmer than Monterey Bay back in California. Because I was wearing a suit and tie beneath the dry suit and not something a bit warmer, I was surprised at how warm I was. I knew most people didn't bother with wetsuits at all out in the Caribbean, and the one time I'd scuba dived in Jamaica, I'd just worn a t-shirt and board shorts, but it was still shocking.

Since I hadn't put any air into my dry suit to provide buoyancy, I plunged beneath the waves. A few moments later, I kicked my legs a couple times and hit the button on my chest to move some air from my tank into the suit itself. A second later I'd stabilized myself about fifteen feet down. I took a moment to grab my flashlight off my hip and flick it on. The beam sliced through the darkness, giving me a lance of narrow visibility.

I hadn't known what to expect given the churning sea, but I was immediately thankful the water wasn't cloudy. Even still, my heart hammered in my chest as I swung the beam in a slow circle, on the lookout for sharks. That was the thing about the ocean, there were always sharks around, and just because you just couldn't see them from the surface didn't mean they weren't there.

Satisfied none were close enough to take a bite out of me, I crossed my arms over my chest, while holding my light to illuminate my path. I began to kick with slow, straight-legged efficiency, allowing my fins to do most of the work, while I balanced and tried to breathe as steadily as possible.

My oxygen use began to slow. A quick glance at my gauge let me know I had about thirty minutes of air in the tank. Still that was counting the lungfuls I'd gulped when I'd jumped in, and what I was using for my suit, so I likely had a bit more, especially since the water was warm.

I took another swallow of air, marveling that I was underwater and nearly weightless as my GPS pinged to let me know I was heading toward the target. By my estimation, it'd only take me about fifteen minutes to swim the quarter-mile or so. Granted that was a bit slower than my old training days where I'd do a whole mile in forty-five minutes, but I didn't want to waste unnecessary energy on the way there.

Half of survival was being less tired than the other guys. Once I got on that ship, there were going to be a whole hell of a lot of other guys.

Still, I couldn't focus on that now because I was fast approaching the boat. Part of me had hoped I'd find some sort of makeshift dock attached to the Hard Tide for easy boarding, but not only did I not see anything like that, but I couldn't find any other boats in the water nearby. Evidently, everyone had gotten aboard some other way. That was going to make getting aboard difficult, especially since I didn't see an anchor chain in the water I could climb up.

I cursed, wishing I had a grappling hook or something, but there was no such luck. I kicked hard, aiming toward the back of the boat. Even with my fins, it was going to be hard to keep up with the boat, and I was glad the hundred foot yacht didn't seem to be moving very quickly.

"Someone up there must like me," I mumbled as a pink line flashed in the beam of my flashlight. They'd thrown down a trail line for people to grab in case they fell off. It was common enough because even the strongest swimmers could get carried away by the current if they fell off, but I hadn't expected it.

Guess someone was looking out for me. As I swam toward it, I grabbed hold of the line and took a deep breath. This was about to get a lot less fun and quickly. I was just glad the boat wasn't that high off the ground.

As I cinched the line to my belt so I could let the boat carry me forward, I pulled off my fins. I held them for a moment before tying them to the line. I wasn't sure if I'd be coming back for them or not, but either way, I felt bad just leaving them in the ocean.

Even holding the line, it was a bit weird to kick in the water, and I could immediately tell how much slower I was going. Guess it was good I was at the boat already.

A couple moments later, I'd pulled off nearly all the gear I could before I disconnected the oxygen tank. I left it all tied to the line and hoped no one would notice it as I clamored forward along the line until my feet touched the sidewall. Then, using strength I didn't know I had, I pulled myself out of the water.

My muscles screamed with the effort as I got my feet up on the side and pulled my happy ass up until I could reach the rungs of the ladder on the side of the boat. I was just glad it wasn't far because if it had been, I'd have been screwed.

Once I was on the ladder, it became exponentially easier, and I hauled myself up. The sounds of the party filled my ears as I pulled off my hood so I could hear better. Then I pulled out my Glock and clambered up. I carefully poked my head up, and seeing no one, I hopped over the side and flopped down on the deck of the ship.

I sucked in a gulp of air before getting to my feet and moving across the walkway toward what looked like a small room. I ducked inside it and found myself inside a bathroom.

After what felt like forever, but was probably only a couple minutes later, I emerged from the bathroom in my suit and tie. I had my Glock holstered beneath my jacket for a quick draw, and my knife was hidden up one sleeve.

The party was boisterous, filled with scantily clad women lounging around a pool while dance music played. Waiters wearing white tuxedos moved around the perimeter carrying flutes of champagne. I wasn't sure which guys were the drug dealers per se, but I was willing to be it was the fat guys wearing gold chains with the women crawling all over them.

A grimace crossed my lips as I glanced around, trying to figure out who was running the show. I couldn't tell, but that was fine. All I had to do was blend in for a while, and I'm sure the host of this little party would make himself known.

Deciding to do just that, I headed toward the bar feeling out of place but doing my best to blend in. It was hard because while the suit I was wearing was nice, it was still off the shelf, and most of these guys looked like their buttons cost more than my entire wardrobe.

Hopefully, no one would notice.

Moving quickly, I found the bar and sat down beside a guy with salt and pepper hair. He wore a tuxedo t-shirt and cabana boy white slacks and had one of those captain's hats on his head. He glanced up at me as he nursed a glass filled with a giant ice cube and whiskey.

"Hello," he said, his big blue eyes taking me in as he raised his glass. "Enjoying yourself?" His voice was surprisingly pleasant, and from the way he spoke, I got the impression he actually cared.

"Yeah, I'm not much into crowds," I said, shifting in my seat so I could look out at the party.

"Not much of a party person either?" he asked, gesturing toward the scene with his glass before laughing and waving at the bartender who had been across the way trying to not make eye contact with him.

"Sir?" the bartender said, coming over so quickly I thought he might leave a dust outline behind himself.

"Ted, this man is conspicuously without a drink," the older gentlemen gestured at me before taking a huge swallow of whiskey, draining the glass in a single gulp. He slammed it down on the bar. "As am I, and I'd hate to think we were in the Sahara."

"Sorry, sir, what would you like?" he asked, sweeping the empty glass off the bar and wiping the bar with a rag that seemed to have materialized in his hand.

"Something nice," he said, glancing at me. "Say, you drink whiskey, son?"

"When it's good whiskey," I replied, eyeing him carefully. Something was definitely off with the guy, but I wasn't sure what. "I'm not a fan of the cheap stuff. It might go down around a hundred proof, but it comes up two hundred proof, if you know what I mean."

"I hear that," the guy said, gesturing to Ted, the bartender. "Why don't you break out the Dalmore 64?"

"The Trinitas?" Ted asked, mouth falling open in shock. "Are you sure?"

"I don't seem to recall myself stuttering," the guy next to me said, rubbing his chin. "Was

I somehow unclear?"

"No, sir. Right away, sir." Ted nodded furiously before rushing to the other side of the bar and disappearing through an alcove.

"Dalmore. I've heard of that. It's supposed to be pretty good, right?" I asked, raising an eyebrow at him. "I think I had a Dalmore 15 before." I shut my eyes, remembering how smooth it had been. The stuff had been so amazing, I'd been surprised to find it was one of Dalmore's cheaper whiskeys even though it cost almost a hundred bucks a bottle.

"You have no idea," the guy replied as Ted returned with a stag's head emblazoned in in silver along with the words Dalmore Trinitas. It looked to be nearly full, and I watched as Ted plunked down a huge ice cube in a glass before pouring two fingers' worth in a glass.

"Is that enough, sir?" Ted asked, holding the bottle like he was afraid he might drop it.

"This is fine," he said, reaching out to take the glass. He held it up, inhaling the scent before handing it to me. "Consider it a gift." He glanced at Ted. "Pour one more, but add a splash of water please."

"Of course, sir," Ted said, glancing from the man to me and back again. It'd only been for a second, but I could feel a mixture of fear and jealousy in the bartender's eyes.

"To your dad," the man said taking his glass from Ted and holding it up to toast. "May we eventually find him." My blood ran cold as he tilted the glass back and took a sip. "Go on. It's bad luck not to participate in a toast, Billy."

The next minute or so happened in a blur. I stood, going for my Glock as he sat there sipping his Dalmore. As my hand disappeared beneath my jacket, a dude who would have made a professional wrestler look small grabbed my left shoulder and spun me around. My hand flew from my coat sans gun as his meaty fist came at my face.

I ducked, allowing the attack to pass overhead as I buried an elbow in his side. He buckled forward as my knee came up onto his crotch. His eyes bugged out of his skull right before my heel lashed out, shattering his knee.

He collapsed to the ground as something hard smacked against the back of my head and everything went black.

CHAPTER 26

I woke with a splitting headache, and as I tried to move, I realized I was tied to a damned chair. I struggled anyway, feeling the nylon rope cut into my wrists as I struggled. My flesh would give long before the ropes even thought about it.

"I'm glad you're finally awake, Mr. Ryder," the guy who had offered me the drink said. He wasn't wearing his jacket anymore, and his white shirtsleeves had been rolled up to reveal well-muscled forearms as he leaned over the backside of a chair. "I'd like you to meet my acquaintance." He gestured toward the left where a guy with a handlebar mustache and a cowboy hat sat on a bench beside a bunch of power tools. He had one leg kicked up on his knee, giving me a good look at his leather cowboy boots.

"Howdy," the cowboy said, nodding toward me as one hand went up to the brim of his black Stetson.

"What's going on?" I asked, surprised I wasn't beat to shit yet, but judging by the cowboy, the best was yet to come.

"See, I have a problem," the guy said, smiling at me. "I need to find your dad. He's disappeared with something very important to me." He sighed. "I need it back."

"Wait, you don't have him?" I asked. That was nearly the best thing I'd heard all day. If these guys didn't have my dad, then he was out there somewhere.

"If I had him, you'd be dead already." He gestured at me. "I'd have just shot you and thrown you into the ocean for the sharks." He sighed, getting to his feet and sauntering toward me. "As it stands, I need information, and while I'm fairly certain you don't actually know where he is, I'm hoping we'll get a good idea." He reared back and slugged me across the face.

My head snapped to the side in a spray of blood as pain shot through me. Stars flashed across my vision, and as my head started to fall back into place, he knelt down in front of me, grabbing my chin between his thumb and forefinger.

"I don't actually like hurting people," he

said, turning my head so I could see the cowboy. "That's why I have Jimmy. He likes it a lot."

"Good to know," I said, before spitting a gob of blood in the man's face. He slowly reached up to wipe his eyes with his hand. He stood and sighed.

"It really doesn't have to be like this," he said, turning on his heel and heading toward a door. As he did, he waved one hand over his head. "Jimmy, let me know when it's done. I want to see to his two friends." He quirked a smile at me over his shoulder. "Your girlfriend seems very nice. I'm going to have to arrange some alone time between the two of us, if you know what I mean." With that, he exited through the door, leaving me alone with Jimmy.

Burning rage exploded through me. If he hurt Mary Ann, I'd...

I didn't get to finish that thought because Jimmy belted me across the face with the back of one hand. Again my head snapped backward, but this time, instead of letting me rest, he slugged me in the stomach. It hurt. A lot.

"Pay attention," Jimmy said, turning toward the bench and picking up a hammer and a knife. "You can get the one or the other. I honestly don't care." He smirked. "That's a lie, I like the knife a lot more." He drove it into my thigh.

Pain raged up from the wound like wildfire, setting every nerve ablaze. My jaw tightened, biting down the scream that threatened to tear from my throat as I jerked violently, trying to get away even though I was bound tight.

"How's that feel, Mr. Ryder?" he asked, wrenching the knife around in my flesh before letting go and standing. He held the hammer out to me and smiled. "See, here's the thing. The boss wants information, but I don't care much about that. So talk or don't. It's fine with me either way." He moved down, pulling off my right shoe and flinging it across the room. "Actually, don't talk. You'll need to save your voice for screaming."

"That's good to know," I said as he raised the hammer in the air, ready to smash my toe into bits. As the hammer fell, his head exploded into a fine red mist, drenching me in blood and thicker bits. His headless corpse collapsed to the ground, his hammer striking the ground beside me with a clang.

Tom, the guy who had come by the house earlier, stared at me from behind the barrel of a smoking gun.

"You sure do know how to make an entrance, Mr. Ryder," Tom said, moving over to me. He jerked the knife from my leg and used it to cut me free of the ropes. It felt like it took forever, but that may have been due to the throbbing in my leg.

"Thanks," I mumbled, and as I spoke, he turned to go

"It's not a problem." He glanced at me over his shoulder, barely a shadow in the outline of his door. "Remember the deal. If Mandrake doesn't go down, I won't help you find your dad." With those words, he left, leaving me all alone in the room.

I nodded and got to my feet. My leg burned. Blood gushed from the wound, making my pantleg stick to my flesh as I trudged forward with my good hand on the guardrail. As I reached the door, I realized it led to stairs that went up toward the outside.

Gritting my teeth, I tried to ignore the pain, and the blood making my foot slosh in my shoe. Everything was secondary to the wound though. I could feel it throb beneath my pants.

I was bleeding, and with every beat of my aching heart, blood gushed from the wound. I could feel it run down my leg and soak through my sock so I left bloody prints on the dirty floor.

I took a step off the stairs, and my dress shoe slipped on the slick steps. The world went topsy-turvy as my feet went out from under me. I reached out, desperate to grab onto the railing, only my leg was slashed open. Agony tore through me as my bloody fingers grabbed for the handrail… and missed.

Then I was flat on my back. Bright lights danced across my vision like stars on a windswept night as the moon glared down at me from the sky above. Warm Florida ocean spray splattered across my face as I stared up at that moon, and my breath caught in my throat.

I tried to wipe my face, tried to make myself move.

Only I couldn't. I was too old, had lost too much blood, and even with Mary Ann, Ren, and my dad counting on me, maybe enough was enough.

The one thing I did know was this though.

This old Marine was too damned stubborn to die. Not when he had a job to do.

I rolled myself to my hands and knees, ignoring the dirty water seeping into my slacks. I was still wounded, and as I stared down at my leg and watched the bloody puddle spreading outward around it, I knew I had to stop the bleeding.

Fortunately, I could do that.

I picked myself up and stumbled back inside. Those bastards might have taken Mary Ann, but even if they hadn't, if there was one thing I didn't like, it was a bunch of goddamned thugs thinking they could do whatever the hell they wanted in my town.

And, much as I hated to admit it. This was my town.

CHAPTER 27

I ground my teeth together as I propped my leg up on the chair and used the dead man's undershirt to staunch the bleeding in my upper thigh. So far, no one had come inside to look for me, but I had no idea how much longer I had. Sooner or later, someone would come. Worse, I had no weapons other than the knife that had been in my leg.

As I sat there, seconds turning to minutes, I focused on being calm. They had Mary Ann and Ren, and while I wasn't sure how everything had gotten FUBARed, I had to save them. Then I had to kill Mandrake so I could get the location of my dad from Tom. It seemed impossible, but I was going to try anyway.

Satisfied my leg wasn't bleeding anymore, I

tied the makeshift compress in place with some of the ropes they'd once bound me with and made my way back outside. My leg hurt like a son of a gun since most of the shock had worn off, but that was fine, I could handle a little pain. This time, I made it outside easier, and as I grabbed at the handrail and pulled myself onto deck inch by painful inch, I could hear the sounds of the party in full swing.

"So they kept partying while leaving me for dead," I grumbled, suddenly incensed. I had half a mind to go out there, guns a blazing, but I didn't have a gun. Well, it was time to change that.

I made my way toward the back of the boat where I'd stashed my stuff. Each step sent a jolt of agony through me, but I fought the pain as best I could, focusing on how much I was going to enjoy seeing the look on Mandrake's face as I choked the damned life out of him. Probably more than was proper.

As I approached the bathroom I'd used to change, a waiter dressed in a white suit carrying a platter laden with food too expensive for me to know on first sight ambled into my path. His eyes widened in shock as I lunged forward, my fist arcing through the air. My knuckles caught him under the chin, knocking him on his ass.

His platter hit the ground next to him with a clang that was mostly muffled by the sounds of the party, and as he lay there dazed, I grabbed the metal platter and smacked him in the face. The crack of his nose shattering filled my ears as he dropped to the ground unconscious. I took a deep breath, not sure what to do with the man as I looked around for somewhere to hide him. The smart move would be to drop him overboard, but that just rubbed me the wrong way.

Instead, I grabbed him by the ankle and dragged him toward the bathroom. Satisfied he wouldn't immediately be seen, I opened the bathroom door and saw, much to my delight, my bag was still sitting in the corner where I'd left it. I hastily reached in and grabbed the block of C4. Hefting it in one hand, I grabbed my spare gun from the bag and made my way outside again.

I headed toward the engine room, small stabs of pain jabbing my leg. I clenched my jaw, trying to ignore it as the party continued on the other side of the boat. I had no idea where my friends were, but I knew I had to find them. The best way to do that would be to find someone in the know and beat it out of them. Unfortunately, I also couldn't risk the Hard Tide getting away.

No. I had to make sure she went down. If not, my dad would be lost. So the engine room it was.

I readied my Glock and moved forward,

and as I did, I saw a man dressed in black slacks and a black turtleneck smoking a cigarette. He stood next to a metal door that appeared to lead into the depths of the ship. Perfect.

"So, where might a guy find the engine room?" I asked, pressing the gun to the back of his neck. He stiffened, the cigarette falling from his fingers and into the choppy sea below.

"You're a dead man," he said, not bothering to move as he stared out at the churning sea.

"Yeah, I hear that a lot, but somehow I'm still kicking," I ground the gun into his skull. "Now, am I going to have to toss you overboard or are you going to help me."

"The engine room is through the door behind you. Follow the corridor to the stairway at the end and head all the way down." He planted his hands on the guardrail. "Seems, I have fulfilled my end of the bargain."

"It seems so," I said, pulling back a step and keeping the gun trained on him.

"So, you're going to let me go?" he asked, slowly turning to look me up and down.

"Yeah," I said, right before he stepped to the side, left leg arcing out toward me.

I fired, putting a slug right in the middle of his chest. Blood splattered across the railway behind him as he stumbled toward me. He looked up at me, and as the report of the gunshot echoed in my ears, I hooked my arms under his armpits to keep him from collapsing to the ground. The light from his glassy eyes faded as I carried him toward the guardrail and hoisted him over.

His body hit the sea below with a splash I couldn't hear, and before he'd even fully submerged, I made my way toward the door.

Part of me wanted to sprint, but I couldn't do that with my leg. Slow would be fast in this case. While I was a touch worried someone had heard my shot, no one had so much as poked their head out of the woodwork. Still, that didn't mean someone wasn't on their way.

The corridor was lit with fluorescent light, giving it an antiseptic feel as I moved along one step at a time. The sound of my own ragged breathing and footsteps seemed to fill the tiny space, making me jumpy, and as I glanced back over my shoulder nervously, I was surprised to find no one behind me.

I continued on like that until I reached the stairs. Thankfully, no one was guarding them, so I quickly made my way down. It was hard, making my leg shriek with agony every time I put weight on it, but I made it all the way down anyway. Thankfully, it didn't go that many steps down, and after only a minute or two I found myself staring at a closed door. Worse it was padlocked shut.

A man dressed like the fellow I'd shot above sat right outside the door in a steel folding chair reading a book.

As he thumbed over another page, I stepped out from cover and raised my Glock.

"Don't make any sudden movements if you want to keep breathing." He froze, mid-page turn, and as his eyes snapped up to focus on me. "I just want to go inside." I gestured at the locked door with one hand. "You think you could unlock that door and let me in? I'd be much obliged if you would."

"And if I don't?" he asked, raising an eyebrow at me as he folded the corner of his book and shut it. "You'll what, kill me?"

"Yes," I said, nodding at him. "That's exactly what will happen."

"Okay," he said, getting to his feet and moving toward the lock. Much to my surprise he thumbed in a code and pulled the lock free of the hasp. He turned, holding it out to me. "Here you go." He dropped it, allowing it to clang across the floor.

"Great," I said, right before I smacked him across the face with the gun. He wobbled, shock and pain filling his features as I drove my elbow into the side of his head. His eyes rolled up in his skull as he collapsed to the ground like a jellyfish.

As he lay there unmoving, I took a step toward the door. It opened easily under my hand, but what I found inside shocked me. Sitting at a card table were two tattooed thugs wearing wife beaters. As they turned to regard me, I noticed Ren laying on the ground beside them. His mouth had been duct-taped shut, and his wrists and ankles were zip-tied together. Worse, he looked like someone had decided to beat out a drum solo on his face.

I shot the two thugs as they started to stand. Putting a round in the left one's face and a round in the right one's chest. They toppled to the ground, their lives reduced to gooey bits of paste that splattered across the machinery behind them.

"You okay, Ren?" I asked, moving close to him and tearing the tape from his mouth.

"Ouch!" he cried, bucking a bit before letting out a breath of relief. "Thanks for saving me." He swallowed hard. "But they took Mary Ann." His eyes looked everywhere but at me. "Guess the head honcho had something special in mind for her." He spat as I used my pilfered knife to cut the zip ties and free him.

His words struck me like a knife to the gut, and for a second I couldn't breathe. I'd known they'd had Mary Ann, but I hadn't really thought about what they might do to her. Now that I did, rage exploded through me. I wasn't just going to stop them. No, I was going to rip off their heads and crap down their throats. I would make it so they wished I'd never come back to town. If they had touched even a hair on her head, I would take everything from them. Everything.

I dropped the pouch with the C4 on the ground beside Ren. "Let's throw a wrench in their plans." I gestured to the machines, not quite sure what all the gears and whatnot did. "Can you do something they won't like with that?" I pointed to the C4.

"Sure can," Ren said, rubbing his wrists. "Just give me a few minutes." I nodded, and he moved over to the satchel and pulled out the C4. "Why don't you go watch the door? Because now that I'm looking at things, I wanna do something that will really blow their minds."

"Sure thing," I said, leaving him smiling like a kid in a candy store. "I'll let you do your thing."

CHAPTER 28

"All done," Ren said, coming out a few minutes later. He shut the door behind him as he shot me a toothy grin and held out the detonator. "One press of this button and these guys are going to have a very bad day."

"Great," I said, rubbing my face with my hands. I was leaning against the wall, trying to take some of the weight off my leg. Somewhere over the course of my getting Ren freed, I'd started to bleed again. Not enough to worry me, but enough to know I was definitely going to need stitches to get it to permanently stop.

"You don't sound as excited as I thought you'd be, Billy," he said, clapping me on the shoulder. "Is it because of Mary Ann?" As he spoke, his smile darkened around the edges. "Because she's a tough girl. I think she'll be okay until we find her."

"Yeah, about that," I said, shoving my tired body off the wall and looking him in the eye. "I need you to take off and blow the Hard Tide sky high as soon as you get to the maximum range." I gestured to the engine room.

"You can't be serious, Billy." Ren shook his head in disbelief. "If I do that, there's a good chance you'll die along with this yacht. 'Sides, I wanna help, and trust me when I say you'll need it."

"I believe you," I huffed, running a hand through my hair. "But I can't have you dying for me." I reached out my free hand to him. "And I need this boat to go down. I know you can do that."

"You're not making any sense. Who blows up a boat while still being on it?" he asked, staring at my hand like he'd never seen one before.

"If the head honcho goes down, a special agent named Tom will give you the location of my dad. I'll send you his picture so you can make sure you can find him. Hear me when I say I need to make sure someone finds him afterward. Otherwise, all this," I gestured around us, "will be for nothing. I will get Mary Ann to safety, don't you worry about that, but just in case I don't get there, I need you to find him, okay?"

Ren swallowed hard and stared at his shoes

for a moment before looking up at me and sighing. "Okay." He took my hand then. "Good luck, Billy. And try not to be a hero."

"That will be easy," I said, shaking my head. "I ain't no hero, just a Marine trying to do his duty and take out a few bad guys along the way."

"Oorah," Ren said, nodding at me. "Well, don't let me keep you."

With that, we made our way back outside. I kept expecting people to leap from the shadows, but none did. It was sort of surprising, but then again, I was pretty sure Mandrake thought he had this all sewn up. He was probably back on the deck, drinking his stupid Trinitas.

The Florida air outside hit me like a damp breath, and as I inhaled a lungful, I tossed a glance sideways at Ren. "So how do you figure on escaping?"

"They didn't sink your dad's boat or anything," he said, gesturing toward the sea. "It's tethered out there." He pointed into the darkness. "There's some kind of oceanic dock thing. Once they had us captured, they drove the boat there and tethered it." He grinned at me. "Don't worry, I'll get there." He looked me up and down. "Just tell me where your fins are."

"I left them at the end of the trail line at the end of the boat. They're probably still there."

He nodded. "I really hope that's true," he muttered before walking away toward the back end of the boat, hands shoved in his pockets. "By the way, I can't exactly get the detonator wet. I'll set a timer for fifteen minutes. That should be enough time for me to reach the dock. You have until then before this whole side of the yacht gets a hole where it really doesn't need one."

"Roger," I said, partially wanting to follow him to make sure he'd get back okay, but I knew he didn't want me to. If he had, he'd have told me. Ren wasn't exactly the type of guy who wouldn't ask for help if he thought he needed it. "Good luck."

"Same to you, Billy. Seems you'll need it a lot more than me."

I couldn't argue that as I turned away from him. Besides, it was time to finish this. My grip tightened around the Glock in my hand as I checked it over once. Satisfied, I moved forward, taking quick, careful steps that shuddered through my body. I could practically feel the flesh around my wound scream with each movement. Still, I didn't have time to worry about that. Not now, anyway. I only had a few minutes before all hell broke loose.

Well, it was time to make the best of it. I moved forward, inching my way toward the party, and as I did, I spied a hallway to my left.

My eyebrow quirked up as I took it in. I hadn't noticed it before, but that was likely because the door had been shut. Now it was open, cracked enough for me to see into the darkness inside.

Something about it was definitely off, and as I stared into its depths, my gut tightened. I wasn't sure what was down there, but I knew I needed to look. I carefully pushed the rest of the door open, while keeping my Glock ready so I could drop any scum bags who might want to put a hole in me.

As the door opened, it revealed darkness and little else besides expensive, cherry-wood panels, and not with the cheap stuff, either. No, this hallway cost a lot, and no one would spend that kind of money on some random hallway. This hallway led somewhere important.

I crept forward, trying my best to see in the darkness. Part of me wondered why no lights had been flipped on, but since there was a small trail of illumination along the bottom of the walls that reminded me of emergency lighting, I was starting to think that maybe the main lighting wasn't working. That struck me as odd though. Wouldn't the party have stopped?

That thought barely entered my brain when the shadows in front of me started to darken unnaturally. I whirled while throwing myself deeper into the tunnel. Agony shot through my shoulder blades as I landed hard on the floor, gun raised. A man the size of a gorilla stood just a few feet away, body half shrouded by a doorway I hadn't seen. He had a monkey wrench raised like he had been about to bat me a good one upside the head.

I didn't give him the chance. I fired the Glock. The crack of the shot practically blew out my hearing in the confined space. My bullet caught him in the shoulder, spinning him around as the monkey wrench slipped from his grip and hit the ground with a heavy clang.

He cried out in pain as I scrambled to my feet, adrenaline surging through my veins. I was on him a second later, tackling him to the ground and jamming my gun under his chin. Crimson spread out beneath him on the tile as I clamped a hand over his mouth. Couldn't take a chance on him yelling for help if nobody had heard the shot.

"I could have killed you, but I didn't." I pushed the gun harder into his flesh, and he squeaked eyes going wide, probably because the barrel was still hot. "Now, tell me where I can find Mary Ann. She has black hair and is about five and a half feet tall. I'm going to remove my hand now, and if you scream, I'm gonna just shoot you, got it?" He nodded, and I slowly pulled my hand away.

"I have no idea what you're talking about," he said through clenched teeth. "I just fix stuff on the boat." He tried to nod overhead but was stopped by my gun. "Lights are out in here if you haven't noticed."

"I noticed," I grumbled, sitting up. "Where's this hallway lead?"

"To Mr. Mandrake's personal suite." He swallowed. "Oh, God. He's gonna kill me, isn't he?"

"I doubt it," I said, getting up and backing away. This guy didn't seem like a soldier or a thug. No. He seemed like some poor schlub who had taken a job on the wrong boat. "But you may wanna get off this boat." I glanced at my watch. "I reckon you have about ten minutes before there's no more boat here."

"Wait, are you a terrorist?" he asked, eyes wide.

"No, but your boss is." I made a shooing motion. "Go on, get out of here."

He nodded, scrambling to his feet while clutching his shoulder. I was sure shock and adrenaline were suppressing most his pain down, and I felt a little bad for having shot him. In retrospect, he'd probably just been carrying his wrench on his shoulder or something. Only...

"Say, where's your stuff?" I asked, and he froze.

"Stuff?" he said, a bit confused. "What do

you mean?"

"Your tools. You said you were fixing the lights. Call me crazy, but usually, you don't use a wrench to fix electrical issues." His face darkened, and then before I could blink, he flung the monkey wrench at me. It hit my shoulder, causing me to drop the gun as pain shot through me.

As the Glock hit the ground, he lunged for me, big forearm smashing into my throat. He slammed me backward against the wall, and my head cracked against it painfully. My vision went dark around the edges as his thumb clamped down on my windpipe.

"I'd sort of hoped you'd catch on. Killing like this is always more fun. I'd half thought you'd turn your back on me, and I'd have to stab you in the back. This way, I get to watch the light go out in your eyes." He grinned as I seized his wrist, trying to pull it away, but I might as well have tried bench pressing a whale.

I grunted, trying to breathe as he held me in place. Only it was impossible. My head felt like it was gonna pop and my lungs burned for oxygen, but try as I might, I couldn't break free.

"Any last words, Mr. Ryder?" He raised an eyebrow. "Why I can't wait until I bring you to Mr. Mandrake. He'll probably reward me by letting me have a go at your girlfriend. What was her name? Mary Ann? She's quite the piece..." He licked his lips as my hands fell to my waist, and as I glared at him, my fingertips brushed against something cold and metallic.

Realization shot through me as my hand tightened around the knife. I jerked it up with the last of my strength. The blade cut into his chest in an upward arc, and he screamed, dropping me. I sucked in a breath that felt like sweet relief and barbed wire before lunging forward with the knife, jamming it into his stomach.

His mouth fell open as the blade sank into his gut, and as he reached up for it, I twisted the weapon, pulling it sideways and spilling his guts across his feet. He stumbled then, tripping in his own entrails as he flopped to the floor, trying desperately to stuff his guts back inside himself.

"I'm going to ask you once," I said, bending and retrieving my Glock. Then I wiped the bloody knife off on my pant leg and shoved it back in my pocket. I pointed the Glock at him as blood oozed through his fingers. "Where is Mandrake?"

He didn't respond, body already trembling as he went into shock and collapsed to the ground, leaving me all alone in the hallway. Still, I knew one thing. He'd said this led to Mandrake's personal chambers. That was something I absolutely needed to follow up on.

CHAPTER 29

As I moved down the corridor, the sound of footsteps filled my ears. A hail of gunfire tore through the space in front of me as I threw myself to the ground. Bullets chewed an erratic path through the wall behind me as I landed hard on my elbows. My Glock came up, and I fired a couple quick shots as I rolled sideways toward the other wall like I could somehow scrunch myself into the wall itself.

The gunfire stopped as my assailant took cover in an alcove just ahead. That wasn't good. Not only did this guy shooting at me mean my cover was likely blown, but worse, if I got bogged down in a firefight more people would come.

Silence descended over the corridor in the wake of the gunfire as I squinted into the darkness, trying to find my attacker. A gun barrel glinted in the low light, and I fired on instinct. A cry filled my ears as I heard someone collapse to the ground.

I scrambled forward, gun at the ready while being careful to stay low. The guy was only a few feet away, and as I saw him trying to breathe through a ruined throat, my blood ran cold. He'd been nearly on top of me. That wasn't good. If he'd have shown up ten seconds earlier, I'd have been dead.

"Thanks for the gun," I send, bending down and picking up his AR-15. I hefted it in my hands as I slid my Glock into the holster. Then I moved forward. Part of me wanted to check on the guy, but even if he could somehow survive a bullet to the throat, which I doubted. Not with the amount of blood gushing between his fingers. He'd be in no position to stop me.

I crept forward, staying low, and as I did, I heard footsteps ahead of me followed by a door slamming. It wasn't far away, and I fired my assault rifle even though I couldn't see anything in the gloom.

A cry filled my ears, and I charged forward, emptying the weapon as I did so. I dropped it and drew my Glock as I came upon the closed door. The body of a guard lay against it, his chest torn open by gunfire. I pushed the sight of his slack face out of my mind as I relieved him of his AR-15 and stood.

I took a deep breath and held it as I leaned into the door, listening. Inside I could hear movement. Part of me wished I had a grenade or something to lob inside, but what if Mary Ann was inside? I couldn't just go all guns blazing.

I pushed on the door. It didn't open. Locked.

"Damn," I cursed, eyeing it. Of course, it was locked. Worse, I didn't see any keys on the dead man. That's when I decided I didn't care. I stood off to the side and put the barrel of the AR to the wall beside the locking mechanism and let loose a three-second burst. The bullets tore into the wood around the frame, and as the silence following gunfire faded, I lifted the dead man and pushed him against the door.

Once he was in position, I retreated a few steps before running forward and burying my foot into the space beside the locking mechanism. The wall snapped like cheap kindling as the door swung inward. Gunfire erupted from inside, peppering the dead man as I moved to the side of the door and lined up my AR. A couple quick bursts took out the guard on the left, and as the dead man hit the ground inside the threshold, someone moved forward.

Another three-second burst took care of him. Unfortunately, as my AR went empty, I heard footsteps behind me. Damn.

I took a deep breath, grabbing my Glock as I threw myself inside the threshold. Bullets tore into the space I'd occupied seconds before I landed hard on my shoulder.

Pain exploded through me, and I heard something pop inside myself. Thankfully, shock and adrenaline kept it from doing more than stab me like a goddamned machete.

Breath lurched through my lips as I brought the Glock up only to find myself staring at an empty room. Where was Mandrake?

I stood, confusion fluttering across my face as the footsteps in the hallway grew closer. I moved to the dead guard, using his body for cover and putting my back to the wall as I surveyed the room. There were no other doors in here…

That was all the time I had. A guy moved into the room, crouched low and sweeping the room. I took him out from my spot beside the dead guard, and as his head snapped backward from the gunshot, his partner opened fire.

Bullets ripped into the dead man in front of me as I fired back. My shots found purchase in his flesh, hitting his side and spinning him like a top. Even still, pain bit through my left arm, letting me know I hadn't come away unscathed. Blood gushed from my bicep as I gritted my teeth and brought my right hand up with the Glock and fired again. This time the guy went down with a cry.

I stood there, blood dripping down my left arm to collect on my fingertips before splattering across the ground and looked around. I didn't have a lot of bullets left, and that wasn't good. I quickly holstered my Glock and picked up the dead man's AR-15. It wasn't full, but it'd have to do.

Still, something was wrong. There were too many guards here, and I couldn't imagine Mandrake had set up a trap like this. No, I was missing something.

I took a step forward, surveying the room, and something caught my eye. Most of the walls were covered with paintings. All in that abstract stuff I didn't particularly like, but that I knew took a lot of skill and time to craft.

Only there was one wall that was conspicuously absent from artwork. I crept forward, ears perked to listen for anyone coming, although what with the way my head feeling like it was wrapped in cotton, I didn't know if that'd help much.

As I approached the wall, I ran my hand across it. It gave under my hand, and I pushed. A click sounded from a mechanism, and then the wall popped out, the right side swinging out a few inches. A hidden door with a pressure switch! Glee filled me as I grabbed the edge and pulled it open while being careful to keep myself out of range of incoming bullets.

When none came, I glanced around the corner and found myself looking at a long, gray corridor. This one dead-ended at a pair of stairs about six feet away, leading up through the roof. I moved toward it, and as I did, the sound of helicopter blades revving to speed filled my ears.

I sprinted forward, using my pain, frustration, and fatigue to fuel me. It took nearly everything I had to race up the flight of stairs, and as I surfaced, I found myself staring at a firing line. The helicopter stood about ten feet back, a small black thing with thin metal skin and a pilot already in the chair. Mandrake stood beside the empty door, Mary Ann's bound arms in one hand as he tried to push her inside.

"Mr. Ryder," he said as the three men with assault rifles standing between us stared me down. "You're quite tenacious. I'll give you that. Unfortunately, this is where your little escapade ends."

"Let her go," I said, ignoring the men with their guns pointed at me. They hadn't shot me, but I knew they would the second I made a move.

"Oh, I will," he said, shoving her toward the helicopter. She tried to scream something to me, but the sound was cut off by a hard slap. Her head snapped sideways, and she sagged in

Mandrake's grip. "Once I'm about a hundred feet above the ocean." He grinned at me. "Wonder how well she swims all tied up."

"This is your last warning," I snarled, my vision tingeing in a reddish haze of rage. "Let her go. Now."

"You don't seem to understand how leverage works, Mr. Ryder. See, I have all of it." He shoved Mary Ann into the helicopter. She slid across the metal floor, and as she tried to move, he leapt inside the door.

"Oh, I understand plenty," I said, my hand tightening around the assault rifle.

"No, you don't, but you will." He shook his head and gestured at me from inside the helicopter. "Kill him."

Time seemed to slow down as my gaze flitted back toward the men. As their muscles tightened, fingers starting to depress the triggers on their assault rifles, the bomb in the engine room exploded and all hell broke loose.

CHAPTER 30

Ren must have really done a number on the engine room because a geyser of flame erupted from the back of the boat, and the ear-splitting shriek of tortured plastic and splintering wood filled my ears.

As the yacht split like a cracked egg, the entire boat listed hard, causing the men pointing their guns at me to flail for balance. As their hands shot out, wind-milling for purchase in empty air, I unloaded my AR in their general directions. Bullets ripped through them, spraying bloody chunks back across the helipad. I wasn't sure if they were down and out, but I didn't care. I charged forward, my feet slipping across the surface of the ground as I struggled forward.

The helicopter's rotors screamed as

Mandrake slammed the door shut. I raised my AR and pulled the trigger at the metal beast. Unfortunately, as the whirlybird began to lift from the dying yacht, no bullets came out of my gun. I swore, tearing after it. Wind buffeted against me, fighting my every step as the helicopter lifted into the air and turned. The tail swung toward me, and I ducked under it, throwing myself toward the landing gear.

My hands wrapped around the foot of the helicopter as it lifted into the air, and I was immediately surprised by two things. One, it hurt like a mother to hang on like this, and two, there must have been something about the wind generated by the blades because it was a lot easier to hang on than I expected.

As we lifted high into the air, I threw one arm around the foot, wrapping the crook of my elbow around it before throwing my other leg over the foot. I hung there, trying to catch my breath as fire ripped apart the Hard Tide. Already the Florida sea was doing a number on the boat, beating it ceaselessly with waves. As I watched people trying to escape into lifeboats, I hoped Ren had made it. I didn't see the ocean dock he had claimed was there, but at the moment, I had other problems.

The helicopter surged forward, cutting through the air above the ocean and heading back toward the coast. I wasn't sure how long it would take to get there, but judging by how quickly the coastline was coming into view, I knew it couldn't be long.

I stiffened my spine and clenched my jaw as I hauled my happy ass up on the foot of the helicopter. Once I was satisfied I wasn't going to fall to my doom, I drew my Glock. Then I took a deep breath to steady myself and counted backward from three. As I reached one, I grabbed the door and slid it open. A big man with a machine gun started to move, but my Glock ended that business. A pair of bullets caught him in the face, turning his skull into red paste.

As he slumped forward against his harness, I stepped inside. Mary Ann was lying on the ground, and as she caught sight of me, her eyes went wide with terror, and she jerked her head down.

I dropped as the cabin door opened and Mandrake sprayed the inside of the cabin with bullets. They ripped into the metal behind me, and as ricochets bounced around me, the helicopter started making wheezing coughing sounds.

As Mandrake, reoriented himself and aimed the gun at me, I pointed the Glock at him and fired. As I pulled the trigger, he fired. My shots tore into his body, flinging him backward into the cockpit as his bullets tore into my outstretched arm, my hip, and my leg. Sheer, unrelenting agony ripped through me, and my vision turned into a kaleidoscope of color and pain.

A cry of anguish erupted from my lips as my Glock went flying from my hand, disappearing out the open door as wind whipped around inside.

Even though the glass windshield at the front of the helicopter was covered in scarlet spray, I could see Mandrake moving in the cockpit. If he got another shot at me, I was done for.

I pulled myself forward, leaving a bloody snail trail on the floor of the helicopter and reached up, grabbing the machine gun from the thug I'd shot. Its strap was caught on his shoulder, but I bit down and pulled with all the strength I had. As it tumbled free and clattered to the ground beside me, Mandrake got slowly to his knees. His shirt was matted against his flesh with blood.

As he narrowed angry eyes and brought his gun around to shoot me, Mary Ann rolled toward him. Her body smacked into his legs as he shot at me, causing him to lose his balance.

The last of his bullets tore into the ceiling, ripping holes in the helicopter and causing moonlight to stream through the machine's skin. That's when we listed hard, and the sound of screaming metal filled my ears.

My hands wrapped around the machinegun then, and I pointed it at Mandrake as he dropped, flopping down on Mary Ann. She squealed in pain as he braced his spent assault rifle against her throat and bore down with all his weight, trying to choke the life out of her.

"Say goodbye to your girlfriend," he cried as I pulled the trigger on the machine gun. My shots caught him in the chest, throwing him backward in a spray of crimson. He hit the control panel.

Sparks leapt from it, and I heard the pilot cry out as the smell of smoke filled my nose. Then we were falling. The helicopter spun as I reached out, grabbing Mary Ann's bound body and pulling her toward me. My back slammed into the roof before we tumbled to the side. My head cracked against the open door before we were sucked outside and thrown into the horizon.

Mary Ann's eyes met mine right before I felt the crushing impact of the water slam into me, driving everything into darkness.

CHAPTER 31

The shockwave of the helicopter's explosion snapped me from unconsciousness as the cold dark of the ocean grabbed hold of me and pulled me down into its depths. My lungs screamed as I swallowed a mouthful of saltwater. I began to thrash even though my entire body felt like it was on fire.

White-hot agony exploded through me as I kicked my legs, trying desperately to get to the surface. I broke free a moment later, still sputtering as I struggled to breathe. Unfortunately, as I sucked in a breath that hurt all the way down, my heart damned near leapt into my throat.

Where was Mary Ann? The last thing I remembered was falling from the helicopter with her in my arms. Only she'd been bound, and she wasn't in my arms now!

I ducked into the depths of the water, trying desperately to find her in the dark, roiling ocean, but I couldn't find her anywhere. I surfaced, my eyes scanning the surface of the waves even though the only light was the moonlight above.

"Mary Ann!" I cried, and as the words left my lips, I heard frantic splashing behind me. I spun as the surf crashed into me, driving me underwater, and as I plunged beneath the surface, I saw a shadowy form a few meters to my left.

It moved sort of like an inch worm, curling into a ball before lengthening as it struggled toward the surface. Realization exploded through my brain. That was how you were supposed to swim when you were bound, and Mary Ann had been bound. Surely it had to be her.

I'd like to say I broke the surface with a few mighty kicks, but my legs and arm were beaten to all get out. It was a struggle to reach the surface, but somehow I did.

After that, I fell into the freestyle swim I'd used so many times before because it didn't really rely on my legs very much. My left arm hurt like a son of a gun, so my form wasn't very good, but even still, I managed my way toward where I'd seen the shadowy form of Mary Ann.

Another wave smashed into me, driving me beneath the waves, but I managed to kick my way back to the surface as claws of agony tried to pull me down into the sea. Once again, I broke the surface. This time I kicked with everything inside me.

Inch by painful inch, I moved closer to Mary Ann, and as I reached her, another wave drove us both beneath the surface. As my lungs burned and my legs threatened to snap off my body, I wrapped an arm around her waist. Her head shot toward me, eyes going wide as we reached the surface once more.

"Give me a second," I said, pulling my knife free of my pocket and slashing her arms free of the bindings. As soon as they came free, she wrapped her arms around my neck, pulling her legs up to give me better access.

As the waves pushed us under again, I managed to cut her ankles free, and as I did, she shot up like a cork. I tried to follow, my lungs screaming for air as she broke the surface.

Only, I knew I couldn't do it. My body hurt like never before—I was used up. I reached out, trying desperately to grab hold of something, anything to pull myself up, but it was fruitless. As my hand clawed through the sea, I began to plunge downward.

Mary Ann dove back down, and as I started to slip down to meet Davy Jones, she grabbed me, putting her hands under my armpits and hauling me upward. Her legs beat ceaselessly at the ocean until we reached the surface.

She flipped, winding up on her back with me on top of her and kicked, driving us backward through the water. Only, I knew it wouldn't matter. She'd eventually get tired, and what's more, I was still bleeding. Sharks would come, and then it would be over.

"Leave me," I croaked, and as I did, she tightened her grip.

"I'll do no such thing, Billy Ryder!" she snapped. "You won't quit on me now, dammit. Now, take off your pants."

"I'm bleeding. There will be sharks…" I tried to pull away, but it was useless. I was too tired. Too hurt.

"Sharks can smell for a long way. If they find you, they'll find me too, even if I left you. No, we're in this together." She kicked harder, pulling us somewhere. "Take off your damned pants."

I sighed, not wanting to give up, but finding it hard to stay awake. I don't know if it was from the ocean sapping my energy, the blood loss, or some combination, but it was suddenly incredibly hard to keep my eyes open.

"I'm sorry," I whispered, trying to look at her, but everything was so dark and blurry, I couldn't find her face as I got my pants off.

"Be quiet, Billy," she murmured, voice like

an angel in my ear as she pulled them from my grip.

"I shouldn't have left you," I mumbled as the darkness encroached. Off in the distance, I could see flames from where the helicopter had hit the sea. At least, I thought that's what it was. Either way, they wouldn't last long. Not with the ocean as violent as it was.

"No, you shouldn't have." I could hear so many emotions in her voice. Pain, sadness, loneliness that it damned near broke me. I was responsible for all of them. "But you did." She sucked in a deep breath. "And you'll have to make up for that."

"I just don't think that's in the cards," I mumbled, reaching up and grabbing hold of her hand with mine.

"That's enough of that," she said, squeezing my hand. "We'll get through this. Just keep swimming, okay."

"I'll try," I mumbled as the moon overhead became pinprick small and the sound of something cutting through the ocean filled my ears. I tried to turn toward it, but found I couldn't, and what's worse, I couldn't see anything at all. Fear ripped up through me in that moment, but it may as well not have because I couldn't move, couldn't even think as the pinprick of moonlight overhead vanished into oblivion.

CHAPTER 32

My eyes snapped open as I tried to sit up. Pain exploded from the length of my body, and I let out a small cry of pain as the machine hooked up to me elicited a shrill cacophony of beeps. My eyes swam over the plain white room around me before falling on Mary Ann. She was sleep in the most uncomfortable chair imaginable.

Her paperback had fallen to the ground and lay splayed there as I tried to figure out what the hell happened.

"Where am I?" I mumbled, looking down at myself. I was wearing a hospital gown and was covered with so many bandages, I looked like a mummy. Everything hurt, and as I tried to move, I realized I had an IV in my arm.

The machines squeaked again, and as I

turned to look at them, a nurse with skin like dark chocolate and short blonde hair burst into the room. She looked me over in the way my Grandma had when I'd stolen one too many cookies before dinner.

"I'll thank you to stop trying to tear out your stitches," she mumbled, moving past the sleeping Mary Ann, pausing only long enough to harrumph at me. "Good woman you got there. Sat up with you the whole time even when I threatened to have her thrown out. Guess visiting hours don't apply."

"She did?" I asked as I went through an entirely strange set of reactions. She was alive, we were alive, somehow, and what's more, she didn't need her own hospital bed!

"You better believe it," she told me, shaking her head. "I suggest your first stop after leaving is to a nice flower shop, with your second being somewhere more expensive." She glanced pointedly at Mary Ann's hand. "Best be putting a ring on that."

"I... um..."

I struggled to find the words to answer her, mostly because I hadn't had the time to properly process things. Everything had happened too fast for it to be good. Still, the thought of rekindling something with Mary Ann sounded damned good, better than good even. Only, that couldn't be now. I needed to find my father, and where was Ren? Did he find Tom?

"Guess it ain't any of my business," the nurse said, moving through her routine and checking me over. "Just like how you got all them bullet wounds isn't my business, although I find hunting accident a bit hard to swallow." She shrugged, waving a hand. "Honestly, I don't want to know."

"Hunting accident?" I mumbled very convincingly.

"Yeah, your friend with the tattoos... he said you guys were hunting gators and there was an accident, speaking of which, he's in the lobby and asked me to tell him when you were awake. Want me to get him?" She looked at me expectantly.

"Yeah, please," I said, and as I spoke, Mary Ann's eyes fluttered open.

As she caught sight of me, a smile spread across her lips and tears filled her eyes. "You're awake. Thank God above," she whispered, coming to her feet. She rushed over to me, bypassing the nurse like the big woman wasn't there at all. She wrapped her arms around me, causing me to cry out in pain.

A blush spread across her cheeks as she pulled back, concern etched across her features. "Sorry!"

"Thank you," I whispered, reaching up to touch her hand. The moment my fingertips brushed her flesh, an electric spark practically jolted through me, leaving me to do anything other than stare at her angelic face. "You saved me."

"Actually, Ren and Tom saved us," she said, kneeling down beside me as the nurse left the room. "They came only a minute or two later. It felt a lot longer, but it really wasn't. They'd tracked the flight of the helicopter and were already on their way." She rested her head on my arm. "We got lucky. Real lucky."

"Yeah," I mumbled, almost unable to believe it. That they had found us by following the trajectory of the helicopter sounded insane, but then again, my dad knew a guy who had fallen off a boat during the night while trying to take a leak. Three hours later, his friend had awoken, and seeing his buddy missing, backtracked the entire course to find him.

"Guess someone didn't want to meet you just yet." Mary Ann patted my hand as she looked up at me. "Which is good because I think you owe me dinner."

"Pick something expensive," I murmured as the door opened, and Ren stepped inside. Aside from the cut above his left eye, he looked picture perfect.

"Glad you're alive. I have a lot of expenses I need covered," Ren said, jerking a thumb at the doorway as Tom came inside. "Since your friend confiscated the laptop."

Tom rolled his eyes before coming forward,

something red and shiny in his hand. "You did a good job, Mr. Ryder," he said, offering me his free hand. I took it, and he didn't squeeze very hard which was good because I couldn't manage much.

"Expect a bill." I nodded to Ren. "From him." I tried to smile, failed, and sucked in a slow breath instead. "Do you have what was promised? You know, about my dad?"

"Yeah," he said, holding up the phone. The screen had cracked into a spider web, but even still I could see a text message flashing on the screen. Only, it didn't make much sense.

"I don't quite follow," I said, looking from the phone to Tom and back again. I shook the device. "What's this? I thought you said you knew where my dad was?"

"Your dad has a GPS. It was missing from the Storm Ryder, but apparently, he started it. This message has a website." He tapped the phone.

"I've had a few knocks to the head. Can you just lay it out for me?" I asked, eyes flitting from the phone to Mary Ann.

"Basically, we can use the code on there to track down your dad. If he still has the GPS, this will lead us right to him," Ren said, coming forward and putting a hand awkwardly on the foot of the bed.

"Really?" I asked, turning to look at Tom. "Why haven't you found him yet?"

"Because this leads somewhere into the Caribbean, and near as I could tell, it's just in the middle of the ocean. There was no way for me to follow up on it since I was in deep cover. Hell, it took everything just to keep Mandrake from finding it." He quirked a smile at me. "That's not a problem now. Only since the mission is over, I can't go and get him. Not my department..."

"Guess we'll be needing a boat then, huh?" I grumbled, turning my eyes to Mary Ann. "You up for a little trip?"

"Why Billy Ryder, are you asking me on a date?" Mary Ann asked, a smile spreading across her face as she leaned down to kiss me on the forehead. The touch of her lips made my heart practically beat through my ribs. "Of course I'll come."

"What about me?" Ren asked, crossing his arms over his chest. "Don't think I'm missing out on the next adventure after everything we've been through." His face soured. "Even though it does mean going on a boat."

"Well, don't wait too long," Tom said, leaving the phone on the table beside the bed before turning to leave. "He's getting farther away by the moment, which makes me think you have some time, but not a lot." With that, he left the room.

"Guess it's time to get a move on," I said, moving to sit up. It hurt like I couldn't believe.

"Yeah, that's not happening for a few days," Mary Ann said, giving me a no-nonsense stare. "I know you're anxious, but I would be surprised if you can walk without tearing open those stitches." She took a deep breath and looked at me like she could see into my soul. "We'll get everything ready, okay? As soon as the doctor clears you, we'll go. I promise."

"Fine," I muttered, knowing I couldn't argue with her, especially since my legs felt like they were on fire. Didn't mean it set well though.

"Don't worry, Billy. We'll find him soon. I know it," Mary Ann said, taking my hands in hers, and the weird thing was, as I looked at her bathed in the harsh fluorescent glow of the hospital light, I believed her. Now that we had his GPS, we would find my dad. I knew it. But only if I healed enough to go get him.

CHAPTER 33

"Are you sure you're up for this?" Mary Ann asked, glancing at Ren as he slid himself onto the bench inside the Storm Ryder.

"He's the one who just checked out against doctor's orders, and you're asking me?" Ren replied, glancing at me as Mary Ann helped me into the boat. It was tough, every movement pulled at my stitches, lancing me with pain, but it was a good pain, a pain I knew meant the wounds were healing.

Still, we were about to find my Dad. At least, Tom thought we were about to find him. In the six hours since I'd acquired his GPS locator, I'd gotten hopeful that we might see him again. It seemed crazy to think it might all be over soon given what I had to do to find him, but at the same time, I was glad it had worked out.

"He isn't going to throw up all over the boat," Mary Ann replied as she helped me into the cockpit. A fresh stab of pain jolted through my legs as I gripped the wheel. Part of me felt bad because once again Mary Ann was going to be responsible for the rigging, but there was no other way, at least, not if I wanted to find my dad soon. I needed help, and Mary Ann was willing to provide it. What more could I ask for?

"Look, after everything we've been through, I want to be there when we find Billy's dad." Ren crossed his arms over his chest. "If I have to throw up a few times to do that, so be it."

"I appreciate it," I said as Mary Ann slid away from me and began taking off the dock lines. "Everything, really, Ren. You're a good friend."

"I know. It's crazy how little you deserve me." He nodded at me, a stupid smile plastered across his face. Then he leaned his head back and stared at the sky. "But seriously. I'll be glad when this is all over. I like excitement and all, but this." He gestured up at the sky. "The sky, the surf, the sun on my face. This is my jam."

"Is that so?" I asked as I got ready to start the engine. Only before I did, a thought crossed my brain. "Say, Mary Ann. Would you check the thru-hull?"

She glanced at me for a moment before nodding. "Yeah, I better do that since you're an invalid."

A moment later, she flashed me the thumbs up before leaping onto the top of the boat to ready the rigging.

Satisfied, I bent down and started the engines. Just doing that was hard, but that was fine. Pain was nothing when it came to finding my dad.

The next few minutes dragged by at a snail's pace, and by the time I finally pulled out of the docks and was heading past the breakwater, I'd nearly gone insane from waiting. It was crazy because we had a few hours of sailing to reach my dad's location, but I still wanted to be doing something.

"Looks like the wind is with us," Mary Ann said as she pulled on the mainsheet, hauling up the mainsail. The wind caught it, pulling us forward, and I instantly knew we were gonna make it with good time. We were straight downwind, and glancing at the Garmin GPS, a smile crossed my lips. We were already going eight knots. The wind whipped back, hitting me in the face and ruffling my hair as Mary Ann hauled up the headsail, and from the look of the telltales, I knew everything was going to be fine.

Hell, I barely had to try to keep the sails from luffing. Nope, no wrinkles at all.

"We're gonna make great time," Mary Ann said, flopping down next to me and shooting an infectious grin at me.

"I know. It's like the first thing that's gone right in a while," I said, wondering if I should motor while sailing. It probably wasn't necessary, but I was still anxious to find my dad. I mean, sure we had his location because of the GPS tracker, but for all I knew he wasn't at the end of it.

No. I couldn't think that way. Tom had promised we'd find him at the end, and I had to believe him. If I didn't, everything we'd done would be for naught, and I couldn't have that.

"Yeah..." I mumbled, glancing down at the engine. The urge to turn it on was so strong I could barely see past it.

"Billy," Mary Ann said, following my gaze. She touched my arm, trailing her finger down my arm. "It will be okay. He's gonna be right where he's supposed to be." She smiled again at me, and I nodded.

"I really hope you're right."

"She is right, Billy. I know it," Ren said, glancing over at us. His face had already gone a little green.

"I'll believe it when I see it," I said as Ren took a swig from his ginger ale.

"Well, if this is how you're going to be, I will not be sitting next to you," Mary Ann said, getting to her feet and moving closer to Ren. "We're on the edge of victory, and it's such a nice day. Enjoy this moment because if you're right, things are going to go to hell fast. And if you're wrong, well, you'll have wasted a perfectly good day."

"I suppose you're right," I said, trying to make myself believe it. Only, I didn't. I wouldn't until my dad was in my arms again. I couldn't lose him, and while I hoped with everything I had that he was, in fact, okay, and at the end of this electronic rainbow, I just couldn't quite shake the feeling the other shoe was about to drop.

Only that was crazy because we'd won. We'd defeated the Scorpions and sunk the Hard Tide. Mandrake was at the bottom of the ocean, and Tom had gotten enough off that stolen laptop to put most of the rest of the Scorpions behind bars for so long that most of them would never see freedom again.

I should have felt like I'd won, but I didn't.

"I know you're worried, Billy, and as much as I want you to try and enjoy yourself, I get it," Mary Ann said, still looking at me. "But it'd be nice if you tried."

"Okay," I said, nodding at her as I tried to do as she asked. She was right after all. I couldn't go any quicker than I already was. I might as well try to enjoy myself or the next couple hours were going to make me crazy.

CHAPTER 34

"Why Billy Ryder, are you smiling?" Mary Ann asked me as she finished tightening the sheet for the headsail and flopped down on the bench. "Because it seems to me you are, and what kind of woman would I be to take that away from you?"

"A normal one?" Ren said right before we crested a wave and hit the water hard enough for it to send a jolt of pain through my battered legs. Saltwater sprayed across the front of the boat, but I ignored it as I watched the onboard GPS. We were minutes away from the location on the Garmin.

"Is that how you think of me?" Mary Ann asked, fixing Ren with a devilish look as she put her hands on her hips. "Cause if so…" She gestured at the sea. "Trust me, if I toss you out, that whistle won't help you."

"I would never try to imply you — "

"There he is!" I cried, interrupting their banter as I pointed to a speck on the horizon. It wasn't big, just a floating orange dot, but I knew that was it. My heart leapt into my throat, and while, I knew that my friends were trying to say something, I was too busy turning toward it to hear them.

As I maneuvered the wheel to line up our bow with the speck, I felt the wind gust up, filling our sails and driving us forward like greased lightning. We cut through the water, hitting the waves at a forty-five-degree angle as we came up over the top of a larger than normal wave, and for a moment, it felt like we were surfing.

We rode the top of the wave, and as it started to crest, I realized we were going over the top. If that happened, it would crash right down on the top of us. I turned the wheel a bit, causing our direction to shift and our speed to slow. The sails ruffled slightly as the wave passed under us and crashed into the sea. Then I spun the wheel back, focusing on the orange dot.

Only it wasn't a dot anymore. It was one of those inflatable life rafts, and what's more, there was someone inside.

"Dad!" I called as the figure in the boat stood up and waved his arms. I doubted he heard me over the waves, but it didn't matter because we were heading right toward him.

As we got closer, I caught sight of the man inside, and my heart practically burst through my chest. It was him! It was my dad, and he looked okay. Well, as okay as one could be after spending several days alone in a lifeboat.

"That's him, Billy!" Mary Ann cried, turning to look at me. Tears rimmed her eyes as she smiled at me. "It's really him."

"I can't believe it," I whispered, my ability to speak practically nonexistent as we got closer to him.

"I knew you'd find him," Mary Ann said, leaping from the bench and grabbing hold of the recovery line. She readied it as I turned on the Storm Ryder's motor and threw the boat into reverse. The boat fought me for a second, motor battling against the sails as Mary Ann tossed the line to my father.

My old man caught the rope and bent down to wrap it around the grommet on his lifeboat. As soon as it was done, Ren and Mary Ann pulled while I tried to keep the Storm Ryder close.

A moment later, the lifeboat bumped up against our hull, and even though I wanted to go to him right then, I did my duty and kept the boat where it was.

"Pleasure to meet you, Mr. Ryder," Ren said, grabbing my dad's outstretched hands and hauling him aboard.

"The pleasure is all mine," my dad replied, voice hoarse as he looked from Ren to Mary Ann. "Thank you for coming to get me, Mary Ann." He gestured at the water. "I like the sea, but not quite like this." He licked his chapped lips and smiled. "I hate to be more of a bother, but would you perhaps have something to drink. I'm mighty thirsty."

"Of course! Let me get you something," she said, tears falling from her eyes and running down her cheeks as she turned and made her way down into the cabin. "I'm glad you're okay."

"Me too," my dad said, watching her disappear down below before coming toward me. "I suppose I have you to thank for that, eh, Billy?" His arms enveloped me in a hug that was surprisingly strong given the way we found him.

My eyes went a little blurry as I hugged him back. "It was a team effort," I said as he broke away. I know how you don't like me trying to be the hero."

"Good. You got that stubborn streak from me, and look where it got me," he said, sitting down on the bench beside me as Mary Ann reappeared with a bottle of water.

"Here you go, Mr. Ryder," she said, twisting off the cap and handing it to him.

"Thank you, kindly," he said, draining most

of it in nearly a single gulp. He wiped his mouth with the back of one hand. "I mean that. I… I'd probably be dead otherwise. Hell, I thought I might be after the Scorpions found me on their boat when I went aboard to get the gang's financial records from Tom." He held up a small USB stick. "He got me off the boat in time, but when I tried to make my way back, the motor broke and the sail ripped off and flew away…"

"Oh, we sank their boat," Ren said, cracking his knuckles. "The Hard Tide is in Davy Jones's locker."

"Really?" my dad asked, raising an eyebrow at me. "Now, that is one story I'd like to hear from the beginning." He pushed me slightly then. "You know, just as soon as I teach you how to sail the old girl."

THANK YOU

Thank you for reading Hard Tide. If you enjoyed it, please leave a review.

Get all the latest updates at JohnnyAsa.com.

Made in the USA
Middletown, DE
20 March 2018